The
PAPER
ANNIVERSARY

The
PAPER
ANNIVERSARY

Dinah Cox

ELIXIR PRESS
Denver, Colorado

Designed by Steven Seighman

ISBN: 978-1-932-41883-5

Library of Congress Cataloging-in-Publication Data:

Names: Cox, Dinah, 1974- author.
Title: The paper anniversary / Dinah Cox.
Description: First edition. | Denver, Colorado : Elixir Press, 2024.
Identifiers: LCCN 2023033361 | ISBN 9781932418835 (paperback)
Subjects: LCGFT: Novels.
Classification: LCC PS3603.O8898 P37 2024 | DDC 813/.6--dc23/
eng/20230724
LC record available at https://lccn.loc.gov/2023033361

First Edition: 2024

10   9   8   7   6   5   4   3   2   1

For Lisa

CONTENTS

The

PAPER
ANNIVERSARY

Tabloid

With some trepidation I stand before you today on the platform in the center of the city square, the box-woods behind me trimmed to a fare thee well, the columns of city hall festooned with velvet banners, to give you the news: caring for your carpet will not help. Replacing old appliances with new ones will not help, nor will minor modifications, nor the elbow grease of spit-shined surfaces. To change the furnace filter on the same day every month is to acknowledge destruction on a global scale, but your steadiness will not help. Keeping a calendar will not help. The daily distractions and disappointments will not cease to matter, only multiply and intensify, clouding windshields with a fog of doubt. (Products made by Procter and Gamble will not help). Saving stray dogs will not save humanity; humanity will not save itself. These are not the burdens associated with masculinity. Theirs are no less trivial, though not always of the home. Think of tire treads, stainless steel containers that fail to regulate temperature, the stench and stains from freshly killed game. The street cleaner will leave a cloud of dust and the oil will flow downhill into gutters and streams, pipelines made safe by government regulation. Poison will come in all forms, though the poison from snakebites can be cured. If you had ten clamshells and you had to divide them between your own household and your next-door-neighbor's, with the stipulation that any unused clamshells would vanish into thin air, how would you divide them? These are the questions that trouble psychologists, now suddenly aware of Western hegemony. Learning about generosity will not help. Those soft photos of the Russian schoolchildren and their farm animals will not help. A famous feminist literary critic stricken by cancer says to plan a dinner party for vegans, but doing so will not help. And the food will be mushy. And the water foul. And another one dead from complications from surgery. And another one penniless. Taking a vacation or staycation will not help. Falling in love will not help. Keeping a journal will not help. Hamburger helper will not help. That Beatles song or that video game where you pretend to be one of the Beatles will not help. Your only help will be your own dumb luck, made dumber by the sunrise, dumber by nightfall, dumb the whole live long day.

Oh, I Know

My cousin—his name is Ted—is afraid of the dentist. I know it's common for children to fear dentists, but my cousin was twenty-four that year. He dropped out of college and became a banjo player, not that he actually knew how to play the banjo. He became a banjo *model*. That is to say, he modeled for print and television ads for a major fast food chain. In the ads, he was always holding a banjo, not that banjo music had anything to do with hamburgers or vice versa, but somehow my cousin became "the banjo guy" at our modeling agency and, to be honest, he looked the part: scruffy hair, fat lower lip, shoulders that said "I like to jam." But he was afraid of the dentist, for unknown reasons, which was why I was holding his hand in the lobby before they called him back to the chair. He had lost his driver's license after failing to pay for not just speeding tickets but also parking tickets, missing taillight tickets, and—saddest of all—jaywalking tickets. I'd reluctantly agreed to drive him.

"It's going to hurt," he said. "Don't make me go back there."

"Nonsense," I said, because I was the kind of person who could get away with saying words like nonsense. Back then, I was also the kind of person who refused to watch all the same television shows everyone else was watching, but I've changed: nowadays, I watch all the same television shows everyone else is watching, but instead of joining in the fun of anticipating each new episode, I pretend not to like any of the characters or plot lines and tell everyone all the shows should be cancelled. "This dentist is very gentle," I said. "You'll be fine."

The truth was I knew nothing about his dentist, but most dentists at least pretended to care about putting their patients at ease. I figured he'd be OK.

"There's something I haven't told you," he said. He was clutching the bottom edge of a "kiddie table" stacked with toys and cardboard books. Fortunately, we were the only ones in the waiting area. "I haven't been to the dentist since I was a child."

"That's nothing," I said. "Your teeth look fine."

"They'll find something in there," he said. "I'm just sure of it."

"Like what?"

"Cavities," he said. "Decay."

"It's not a big deal," I said. I removed his hand from the kiddie table and placed it in his lap. Normally, I didn't touch other people; I'm not one of those close-talking, rub-against-you sorts. He could tell I was giving him special treatment. And although I am ten years his senior, I did not consider myself a surrogate big sister; rather I was more like a reluctant cab driver or surly next-door-neighbor. Even working for the same modeling agency didn't bring us closer together; besides, I also had a real job as a video editor, and I could tell he imagined he'd be able to get by for the rest of his life on his good looks. Anyway, we were not exactly friends. Unfortunately, the fact of the twenty-first century is that friendship itself is on the ropes. People have "contacts," "followers," even "old friends," but they do not have current, reliable friends in the same sense even I did ten or fifteen years ago. At first, I thought it was merely a product of growing older—sharing a bad pizza and commiserating over Astronomy homework lost its charms once you were solidly middle-aged—but later, I realized it wasn't me at all: it was the entire culture. What was once a slow process of discovering common ground through conversations over lunch and the back and forth loaning of paperback books had been reduced to Planned Events scheduled months in advance: no one really wanted to attend these events—and mostly I skipped anything outside of work—but when they did attend these Planned Events, they dreaded them up until the very moment they forced themselves out of the house, after which they engaged in conversations such as:

"I've been really busy."

"Oh, I know."

"Sure wish we had a better president."

"Oh, I know."

"It was good to see you."

"We'll have to get together sometime soon."

Soon turned into never unless you ran into them at the grocery store, in which case you exchanged embarrassed hellos while trying not to get caught inspecting the contents of their shopping cart. This actually happened with my cousin and me, and although he didn't catch me looking, I saw that his shopping cart contained not only Lucky Charms but also Flamin' Hot Cheetos and a gallon of chocolate milk. His mother and my mother were sisters, so I considered telling one of them about my cousin's poor nutrition, but by the time I saw either his mother or my own mother I'd forgotten all about it. Why I'm remembering it now doesn't matter; that's another fact of the twenty-first century: we elevate the trivial so as to soothe our troubled minds. All those photos of baked goods and mountain vistas and patio furniture are there for a reason, and the reason is we're all afraid of dying. That's been true for millennia, but the difference is our ability to chatter away the day with ephemera. These days we're very good at generating words and images, but very bad at reflection. It's not my fault.

"I never floss," my cousin said at the dentist's office. His name is Ted. Did I already say that? The sad part is it's not short for Theodore. His parents just named him Ted. And his last name is Fredrickson. I'm lucky my first and last names don't rhyme.

I tried to tell him that it didn't matter, a lot of people didn't floss and still did fine at the dentist's office, but he was adamant, recalcitrant, even, so that I had to tell the receptionist to give me a minute more with him alone.

"You're too old to be acting this way," I said. "You'll feel better when this is over, I promise."

"Okay," he finally said. "But you have to come with me."

And that is what began my long year of serviceability; every Friday I accompanied Ted to another appointment or political event or tag agency or bakery or recycling center or post office or photo shoot or zoo. Sometimes, this would bleed into the weekend, so that Saturday or Sunday meant I had no choice but to skip my own plans for wasting hours and hours staring aimlessly at the world wide web in favor of taking him to the department store or hardware store or taco stand or basketball game or gym. All this suggests that we became close—something akin to kissing cousins—but in actual fact all these adventures actually drove us further apart. He was needy, I was grouchy, and no one had any fun at all. But we were driven together by circumstance, the first circumstance being his lack of driver's license and fear of strangers, and the second circumstance being my own dumb refusal to say no.

One day—it was a Friday—I picked him up to go to the tire store. Why someone who didn't have a car would need to go to the tire store is another story—really, it's not even a very interesting story; in fact it's a very boring story having to do with a garden cart he was using to transport his Christmas decorations from his living room to a faraway storage shed—but he needed a tire, and, as you might imagine, was afraid to go to the tire store alone. I was in a hurry because I had a meeting at work that afternoon at three. He'd texted me with only a half-hour to spare, and, like an idiot, I imagined this tire selection thing would go quickly and effortlessly, after which I'd be able to deposit him and his tire and his Christmas decorations with time enough to sneak back into work as if I hadn't been gone in the first place. We made it to the cash register, but there was a line. I considered leaving him there, urging him to take the bus home, even forcing him to walk, but I knew he'd just remain in the long, slow line and somehow talk me into coming back for him after my meeting was over, so I endured the ritual of credit card swiping and electronic signature and will this tire fit in our largest bag? It would not. Ted carried it under his arm. By the time we made it back to car, which was, at his insistence, parked in the furthest reaches of the parking lot, it was five after three.

"I have to hurry," I said, sliding into the driver's seat.

"Oh, I know," he said, in the way of the twenty-first century.

I buckled my seat belt and watched him fumble with his. He made a dramatic gesture of defeat—a kind of slumping in his seat with a simultaneous, loud, humming exhalation. I hesitated before putting the key in the ignition, and when his breathing became irregular, I took my hand off the wheel. I turned to face him.

"How's your mom?"

"I've been meaning to tell you," he said. "She died."

His mother, my aunt, had been ill for months, but by no means I had I imagined she was on her deathbed, not even her death sofa. That week, I'd driven Ted to the florist for a bouquet of gerbera daisies, her favorite. And most of the time I remembered to check in on her, to stick my head in to say hello, bring the mail in from the box, help her with a crossword puzzle clue or bring her something from the salad bar. Why hadn't he phoned me when things took a turn for the worse? Who planned a shopping trip for a lousy garden cart tire right after his own mother had just died? What kind of sociopath went on his merry way asking for no-account favors and talking about the weather without telling his own cousin that her aunt—his mother!—was dead? It seemed not just cold, but bizarrely so, as if he had something more to hide.

"Why didn't you tell me?" I said. "When did this happen?"

"I was waiting for the right moment," he said. "I thought we should be alone. And over the phone seemed so impersonal. I'll never forgive my best friend for telling me about his girlfriend's suicide in a text, so I thought I should wait. And I really do need this tire. And you were late for your meeting, so—"

"Forget about my meeting," I said. "When did she die? Did you call my mom?" I figured I must have been the last person to find out. I went through a long list of names—friends and relatives I was occasionally in touch with—and he answered each one in the negative. He'd telephoned his brother in Ohio, but that was it.

"She wasn't even that sick," I said. "Was she?"

"She went downhill fast," he said. "Hospice came too late."

I hugged him, the first time I'd ever done anything like that. Some families just don't hug, and we were one of those families. He was warm and strangely damp, and he smelled like he hadn't showered in a while. I was worried he might start to cry.

"I'm so sorry," I said. "You should have told me when things were getting bad."

"I know," he said. "I thought I could handle it."

I offered to help him inform all the friends and relatives—I took the list of minor celebrities; he took all the stars. I knew my own mother would have a hard time with the news, so I decided to skip my meeting at work and go to her apartment to tell her in person. Ted offered to come with me, but I demurred:

"You have that garden cart to worry about," I said. "And your Christmas decorations."

"Oh, I know," he said. "I'll manage."

When we parted, I knew my taxi-driving days were drawing to a close. Something had changed in him, and I could tell he would find a way to get his driver's license back, even if it meant taking an Uber every day to the Driving Academy where he could start over again, become self-sufficient, gather his courage to face the perils of the world alone. I knew I would see him from time to time at the modeling agency, where I still picked up occasional gigs as a hand model—Lotion! Engagement rings! Salt and Pepper shakers!—and he was still getting all the mileage he could out of the Banjo-thing while he was still young enough to pull it off. My hands, in spite of a lengthy daily regimen of various expensive moisturizing products, were losing some of their marketability.

For a long time, he didn't call or text, and, though I saw him briefly at his mother's funeral and a time or two at the agency, we more or less fell out of touch, though I kept up with his various social media accounts and assumed he kept up with mine. We had several friends in common, and some of them showered him with compliments at the same time pretending not to notice my presence at all, something that bothered me at first, but eventually came to seem like the natural order of things. I wasn't *needy*, I reasoned, and he seemed to require a daily dose of adoration. All of this would have been fine were it not for the front desk receptionist at the modeling agency, a real Facebooker if there ever was one. If the temperature dropped two degrees, she would be the first one to let you know about it. And, like everyone else, it seemed, she fawned over Ted as if he were the fifth Beatle.

The truth was I was glad to be rid of him. I was staying in a lot. I worked. I shopped. I thought about everyone else working and shopping and pretending to have fun. One Friday night, I saw the receptionist from the modeling agency had put up a post that said, "Check out Ted's new Burger World appearance," which, on the face of it, might not have seemed like a big deal, except that same week my hands were appearing in a big, new ad campaign for HandShaker International that had rolled out in a hilarious—well, I thought it was hilarious—commercial during the Super Bowl. Ted's Burger World ad was running in local markets only. And *of course,* just about everyone ever to exist had clicked Like on the still photo of Ted holding his banjo aloft against a backdrop of the whole, big burger world spinning on its axis against a solar system of onion rings and vanilla shakes. So I was feeling a little out of sorts, maybe a little jealous that day when I saw him at the agency, right in front of the tall desk of the receptionist, the president of his imaginary fan club.

"I have something to tell you," he said. "My mom died." The receptionist looked up from her computer monitor, where, I saw, she had three separate windows open: Facebook, Facebook, and Facebook Messenger.

"I know it's hard," I said. I thought about giving him a hug, but finally decided against it.

"I've been having a hard time," he said. "I meant to tell you earlier."

"I should have called you myself," I said. "After the funeral."

"Oh, I know," he said. "You were at the funeral?"

"Of course I was," I said. "We talked for a while afterward. With the clam dip? And I made a joke about the celery sticks. My mother was with me. Oh well, it was a busy day for everyone, I'm sure."

He looked confused, obviously searching his memory bank for what must have been—to him, at least—a very boring social transaction. "I'm sorry it took me so long to tell you," he said. "Everything has been crazy."

I realized then that he'd *also* forgotten about the *first* time he'd told me his mother had died, that afternoon in the parking behind the tire store. He must have forgotten also that I'd helped him out by taking him to the tire store in the first place. Was he on some kind of medication? Or was my presence in his life altogether forgettable? Maybe grieving relatives did this sort of thing all the time, and no one had told me about it. I'd read about people with repetition compulsions of one kind or another, but this seemed different: as if he'd erased all our interactions—such as they were—from his memory and replaced them with some fabricated version of our true and everlasting kinship and good-natured ribbing, the kind of thing you might see on television shows of yesteryear, *Leave it to Beaver* or *Father Knows Best*.

"I know I can always count on you, Rosie," he said. He actually jabbed his elbow into my ribs. "You've always been there for me, just as I have always been there for you. I mean, I've *wanted* to be there for you, when I can. Do you think you could drive me to the bank later? I have some checks to deposit."

"I'm sorry about your mom," I said. "Really."

"Yeah," he said. "I don't know what kind of person I'm going to become now."

"You should learn to play the banjo," I said impulsively. "I mean, really learn to play."

"That might be cool," he said. "I've been playing tennis."

"Tennis is not artistic," I said.

"No, but it's good for you."

"I'll take you to the bank if you want," I said. "Sometime."

We parted ways, and I decided not to confront him with the facts of his memory lapse. I knew cousins were not all that important in the grand scheme of things. Maybe it didn't matter.

We would have resumed our close-but-not-at-all-close relationship had it not been for something else the receptionist from the modeling agency posted online. No one should care about that kind of crap—and mostly I did not—but this particular series of posts had my attention. That day, the temperature had fluctuated wildly, and a tornado watch was on the horizon. She was posting every five minutes or so with local updates about the wind speed and barometric pressure. More notably, she'd invented some fictional characters from the modeling agency, co-workers she was calling "Wonderful Person" and "Neat-o Person." She said she loved working at our particular modeling agency because her vantage point from behind the front desk allowed her to witness the best of what humanity had to offer, something that surprised me, because as long as I'd worked there—longer than she had—I not witnessed anything remotely good about humanity; in fact I had witnessed a very great deal of the opposite.

So that day the cold front and the warm front were colliding, the storm chasers were hitting the highways, and she had another tale to tell about the many modeling adventures of Wonderful Person and Neat-o Person. Wonderful Person, she said in her post, was "having a hard time," and Neat-o Person somehow had reassured Wonderful Person that life would go on, and—this was the important part—she was delighted to see Neat-o Person smile for the first time in a very long while. Again: the best of what humanity had to offer. In this case, the hero of the story was Wonderful Person, though Neat-o Person came off pretty well also.

The tornado watch turned out to be a bust, but all day I could not stop thinking about Wonderful Person and Neat-o Person. I searched the comments for clues to their identity, but mostly people were writing only platitudes such as, "that's wonderful," or "that's neat-o," or "I'm so glad you work with such wonderful, neat-o people." I ran down the list of possible candidates: there was the young, gay guy who made jokes in the stairwell. There was the other young, gay guy who volunteered to help people hang curtains and change the batteries in their smoke detectors. There was the wife of the big boss, who was not at all wonderful and not at all neat-o but certainly imagined herself a paragon of virtue. Before I knew it, I became fixated on this tale of compassion, and, in spite of myself, began to wonder if *I* was, in fact, Wonderful Person and Ted was Neat-o Person, and in fact the receptionist had been making reference to that day in front of her desk when he told me—for the second time—his mother had died.

The next time I went to the agency to find out about a gig, I hung around her desk for longer than I really needed to and asked her about her favorite TV shows. "I love those characters and adore that plotline," I said, evidence, in my own mind, at least, I'd abandoned the misanthropic ways of my past. "We should text one another about our favorite shows," I said, knowing we never would. She seemed surprised.

"Sure," she said. "I didn't know you watched that show."

"I watch all the shows," I said. "All the wonderful shows, I mean."

Just then, Ted came in from the stairwell. I saw that he was crying.

"Burger World is going under," he said. "Too much competition from Fast-Casual."

"No way," I said. "The last time I was there the place was packed."

The receptionist began to cry as well. "It's just that I won't be able to see you anymore, Ted," she said. "I'm going to miss you."

"Another announcement," he said. "I have *four* cavities."

The receptionist began to cry harder now, and I saw that the box of tissues she usually kept on her desk was out of reach on the windowsill. I plucked one from the box and handed it to her. "Cavities aren't that bad," I said. "Especially when they're not even your own cavities."

"It's hard for me to see the suffering of others," she said.

"Oh, I know," I said. "It's hard for us all."

Playing Cards

The vaccine card is not the library card is not the voter registration card is not the greeting card. The Queen of Hearts has been oversold, by now both sentimental and sadistic, the cruel mother who will transform you into a specimen at once too small and too large to fit the through the keyhole of the much-vaunted male imagination. And the King? He is playing you. He is trumping you. Go ahead and pretend he's one of the good ones, but I've seen him asking his buddies to come over to take turns with a cigar while cooking shriveled roots from the garden. All for your dinner, he says, but he's fattening you for slaughter. Is that a cliché? Maybe it is, but it's not your fault. Maybe it is your fault. Maybe he's in a band. Maybe he's into downhill skiing. Maybe he's *interested* in his own *interests*. Whomever he voted for—in the primaries, of course—you voted for him, too.

* * *

It was an easy decision, you said, the right thing to do, just as allowing him "his own space" made sense three month ago but now leads to your never-ending loneliness, a boring malady you expect me to cure. The baseball card is not the punch card is not the yellow card, each one forbidden to all but those in the know. He wanted you to check out a book. He wanted to be the one who wrote it. He wanted you to get vaccinated so that you could spend more time with your friends. He wanted you to have your own friends, maybe a nice married teacher's aide or a first-year student in the veterinary college. He wanted either a greeting card or extra credit for selecting the exact right greeting card. He wanted a gun. He wanted a rope. Once, a long time ago, he said he wanted you.

Put the face cards in a pile—quickly, now, before he comes home. The appointment card is not the index card is not the cardboard box, though all three have proliferated in your pile of important things to do. If you're an organized career woman, a flamingo with a leather briefcase, he'll perform very particular household chores, the ones he might rebrand as artistic. He has begun to call it *The Home*. If, like the gay man on the pharmaceutical commercial, you have trouble managing the intricacies of the television's remote control, he will put you in *A Home*. If your dog chews his sneaker, he will *re-home* your pets, all of them, even the quiet ones not prone to destruction. The vaccine card is not the health certificate is not the pedigree is not the card you carry in your wallet, the smudged record of your fingerprints in case you turn up missing. He says he's your champion, your cheer-leader, someone who swoons at the sound of your laughter. He grows beefsteak tomatoes, puts them in a basket, and gives them to your boss. The recipe card is not the discount card is not the Jack of Hearts. Standing in the entryway to take your coat and hat, he'll warn you of intruders and sabo-teurs. He knows when to call a spade a spade.

Just how long will he be willing to play second fiddle to your first chair flute? He says he doesn't see it that way, but ev-eryone else can see the writing on the wall. The membership card is not the union card is not the credit card. When your underlings see you walking hand in hand, they imagine his hand is larger. They imagine your hand is softer. They imag-ine he's saving up to buy you a ring. The bank card is not the discount card is not the Father's Day card featuring a cartoon tool box and joke about the dad-jokes his dad never tells. Did you hear the one about the woman who had a baby? She was pushing a stroller, but still appeared pregnant. Her body—prick it with a pin as if it were a hot air balloon—was hilarious. The vaccine card is not the gender card is not the business card. *Mr. and Mrs. Meal Ticket*, he said on the phone when you overheard him making reservations. *Mrs. Meal Ticket will be dining alone.* It's been such a long time since he's played pinochle, he says, and he longs to live again inside the smoky haze of memory, a basement free from the sound of your laughter, a sound—remember—he always says he adores. The cue card is not the room service card is not the truth card. It never was.

* * *

The wool card is not the place card is not the gift card enclosed in an envelope. These are the items present at my dinner party, an occasion I'm hosting in your honor. Don't worry, there will be plenty of cheese. When I was fourteen, I played the nurse in *Romeo and Juliet,* also Aunt Em in *The Wizard of Oz* and Rizzo in *Grease.* You see the kind of girl I was. He, too, could see it, better than you could, and although I willingly became his card-carrying competitor, it was you who received the valentine. When they passed out report cards, mine said, *Satisfactory.* Yours said, *Satisfactory.* His said, *Satisfactory Plus.* Plus what-? Plus his tutor gave him a set of flashcards, and he knows everything as a result. He's a Jack of all Trades. I'm the Jill of Clubs, otherwise known as the girl next door who wants so desperately to move away she sets your house on fire. Where's your insurance card? You're going to need it.

Pick a card, any card. The checkbook is not the storybook is not the matchbook. At the homecoming dance, I am the one who polishes your twin thrones. If there are refreshments to be served, I will serve them. And your friend, the second runner-up-? The judges awarded her boyfriend the title of Mr. Hate Crime 2021. That makes her the queen of hate crimes, the princess of the punchbowl stirring soda in a baby's bottle, the only way, she says, to prevent tooth decay in minors. I heard you all went sailing together. A sailboat is not a tugboat is not a ship of fools. Or maybe it is. I think I owe you a thank-you-card. *Dear King and Queen. You're really going places. Please accept my best wishes for a future free from gambling, soothsaying, and commerce.* Here's my calling card. The winning card is not the hidden card is not the trick card. It's true I'm rooting for your ultimate misery. And his. That's the way, he always told me, you're supposed to play the game.

The Moon Landing

S uddenly, the world had become very loud. For weeks, the marching band had been rehearsing only via Zoom, but now they were officially back in action: temperature checks at the door, hand sanitizer stations in every corner, and most impressively, everyone from the woodwinds to the drum-line wore CDC-approved cloth face-coverings featuring the school's clever and classy mascot, Rocket Steve.

Rocket Steve was a throwback, clean-cut with a hint of an acne scar between his nose and upper lip, a bit like the NASA control room masterminds you see in movies, the kind of guy you could count on to cover your shift when your house caught on fire or your wife went into labor. That he wore glasses was meant to encourage academic excellence among the students of Redwood High, but his muscles more than made up for any perceived weakness. Rocket Steve was not just a rocket enthusiast but a man-rocket hybrid, his entire torso made up of combustible fuel. And when he appeared in support of the carbon-neutral and now Covid-free Mighty Redwood Marching Band, he did so with renewed vigor, since he'd been on hiatus all of last spring, through the summer, and most of the fall.

All the musicians were warming up at once, a cacophony of chromatic scales and recognizable passages from the Mighty Redwood Rocket fight song:

Blast-off righteous riding rockets,
Blast-off sun be prouoououd-!
Blast-off to the sound of music,
Blast-off band be louououououd-!"

Violet, who played the trumpet, hated Rocket Steve because he reminded her of all the actual, human Steves she had known: Steve, the drug dealer who tried to get her arrested, Steve, the shop teacher who wouldn't allow her to use power tools, Steve the leading man in the school musical who treated her as if she were an annoying younger sister. In their own ways, the human Steves all resembled Rocket Steve insofar as they appeared approachable and thoughtful but in fact were antagonistic and temperamental. Like hot chocolate gone cold in a Styrofoam cup, they were all sugary sweetness and warm days by the fire until you dared to take a sip: then they were poison.

The morning after the plague—actually, the plague was ongoing, but people were pretending it was over—the morning band practice resumed, and Violet found herself unable to play even a single note on her trumpet. Her mouth, still sore from the recent removal of her wisdom teeth, would not make melody. That she'd been chosen to represent the Mighty Redwood Marching Band at the upcoming Redwood Dazzle Welcome Back to Razzle Socially Distanced Cheese and Sausage Festival did not make things any easier. She was supposed to stand alone on a raised, wooden platform in the middle of the school building. She was supposed to play "The Star-Spangled Banner." She was supposed to demonstrate proficiency and grace, the promise of a new America. When the big moment arrived, she knew she'd be able to play nothing at all.

She pulled out the mouthpiece and restored the trumpet to its case, a small box something like a coffin for a child or elderly pet. Normally, she brought the trumpet home with her to practice every evening after dinner, but that day she decided to leave it in the storage closet adjacent to the band room, a cage-like enclosure remindful of Al Capone's vault. Just as she slid the trumpet case into its designated cubby, the air conditioner began to hum with a soft, menacing, mechanical sound, perhaps the result of the new HEPA filtration system installed in a hurry to protect students and staff from aerosolized droplets now floating in all enclosed spaces. Violet, like most of her classmates, had wanted badly to go back to school, but the constant battle to demonstrate her worthiness for first chair status had made her want nothing more than to return to remote learning, to stay home forever where, thanks to her mother's job as an X-ray tech and her father's job as the manager of a warehouse for frozen vegetables, she often had the house entirely to herself. She had neither siblings nor pets, not since old Pete the pit bull died of cancer. In fact, she was more or less a loner, and some of the people she considered occasional confidantes, gaming buddies she'd met online, she'd never actually spoken to in person. The marching band was supposed to make her sociable, to provide her with "an outlet," to show her parents she, too, could fit in with all the normal teenagers and their "extracurricular activities." She could make YouTube videos on her own YouTube Channel. She could learn songs and then play them backwards. For a long time, she'd thought herself boring, unworthy of even "cool" outcast status among the marching band geeks, but at some point, she realized she was neither boring nor worthless in terms of social capital but merely odd, tragically, tenaciously, unmistakably odd, something she'd inherited from both her parents, people so odd they wore only homespun clothing and kept a collection of butter churns in the basement. And she knew she was an odd child. The only, odd child of odd and increasingly bitter parents. Playing the trumpet wouldn't help. Nothing would.

Violet locked the door to the wooden enclosure housing her trumpet, silent and dead inside its case. She knew she should take it home to practice, but her mouth still hurt from the appointment with the young and preppy oral surgeon, an NRA enthusiast her parents did not approve of, but he was one of only two oral surgeons in town, and the other was said to be an avid consumer of online pornography. That was the way with this town, Redwood, Oklahoma, a town with exactly zero redwoods. Six doctors. Four dentists. Two Oral Surgeons. And about a zillion two-bit preachers who moonlighted as either real estate agents or general contractors. Violet was unlucky to have been born there, unluckier, still, her parents had been too timid to move.

At home that night, Violet noticed her mother's purse— more like a canvas bag meant for groceries than an actual handbag—seemed unusually bulky. What could be inside? She was sure her mother, washing dishes in the sink, would not notice if she looked. Her father was working the night shift at the frozen foods warehouse and would not return until morning. Old Pete the pit bull, her only ally in that house, would have been on the job sniffing out trouble, but ever since that day when her mother, acting in the dog's best interests but not Violet's, made a secret trip to the vet's office to have him euthanized, Violet had decided not to speak, not any more than she had to, anyway, not any more than answering her parents' questions with "yes" or "no." The worst part about her new silence was that they'd hardly noticed, absorbed, as they were, in their own preoccupations, bills that needed to be paid, craft fairs canceled due to the pandemic, butter churns and potato peelers and ancient washtubs that would need to be sold—and soon—on Etsy or EBay.

Violet knew they loved her, wanted what was best for her, but they were so impossibly weird they could not see anything past the petty demands of their own household, a place they seemed to expect Violet to occupy forever, her filial duty overtaking her ambition until she was no longer of marriageable age. And college? Her mother was still paying back her own student loans. Her father said his own parents spent all their money on his older brother's college education and so would not spend one red cent on his. He hadn't wanted to go, anyway, he always said; who needed a bunch of know-it-alls to tell you how smart they were? Instead of going to college, Violet's parents wanted her to take an online course in bookkeeping and go to work where her mother knew someone at Redwood City Hall.

She checked to make sure her mother was still washing dishes in the sink. All these years, and they'd never bought a dishwasher. In fact, her mother would hardly run the water at all. As a result, their dishes were always sticky, their spoons cloudy with stains from yesterday's sour cream. Finally, when her mother began to rinse a roasting pan under the faucet, Violet took her mother's canvas bag from its usual resting place just inside the front door and carried it surreptitiously upstairs.

Indeed the bag was very heavy, and her shoulder hurt from the effort. At the top of the stairs, she grabbed both handles and dragged it the rest of the way to her bedroom. With effort, she lifted the bag onto the rumpled bedspread and impulsively dumped all the contents onto the foot of the bed. Most of it she recognized: car keys, billfold, checkbook, gelatinous and crusty cough drops, half-eaten roll of Life Savers. The file folders held additional boredom along the lines of empty envelopes and letterhead from the radiology center, miscellaneous tax forms, a whole year's worth of credit card bills mixed in with coupons for dog food, no longer necessary, of course, but her mother so loved to save a buck she'd probably use them anyway and donate the impossibly heavy bags of kibble to the Humane Society, where, she was sure, Violet would be made to unload and stack the donations and then demonstrate additional virtue by sticking around to help clean out the kennels.

At the very bottom of the bag, however, was a very large jar, the kind that in its former life must have held mayonnaise meant for commercial sale only. Now the label had been scrubbed off, and the mayonnaise a long-ago memory.

In its current incarnation, it was full of rocks, heavy ones, rubbed smooth and angular, as if they'd been tumbled in a freshwater stream. One of them was in the shape of a heart. Inscribed in the center of the heart was one word: *Steve.*

Did her mother have a secret lover named Steve? She immediately rejected the idea; her mother was strange and socially unacceptable, and she was utterly devoted to Violet's father. Aside from their respective workplaces and occasional craft fairs in neighboring towns, they rarely left the house at all. Downstairs, she heard her mother returning the roasting pan to the cabinet above the refrigerator; the sound was unmistakable because it was the only time her mother ever dragged the stepstool across the floor and cursed. She wondered if her mother ever cursed around Steve. *Shit, Fuck, Damn,* they might say to one another as they pulled into the parking lot at Motel 6. *I hope nobody finds out what we're up to.*

In a hurry now, Violet put all the rocks back in the mayonnaise jar—quietly, she hoped—screwed on the lid, and slid the jar back into its rightful place at the bottom of her mother's bag. She put all the papers back in their file folders and all the coins back in her mother's coin purse, all the cough drops back in what she hoped would appear to be the same random, scattered places they had been before. Quickly, she carried the bag downstairs and tried to make it appear as if her mother had dropped it inside the front door immediately after arriving home from work. In the kitchen, her mother was stacking silverware in a drawer.

"Did you fold the sheets and towels?" her mother asked without looking up.

"Yes," Violet said.

"Did you sweep off the porch?"

"Yes."

"You'll have to prepare dinner," her mother said. "I have work to do downstairs."

She realized, then, her entire evening would be spent chopping vegetables and carrying compost to the yard, stirring mysterious liquids on the stove and scrubbing scum from the sink. She didn't mind solitude and silence, but she did not like to think of herself as subjected to endless toil. No doubt her mother, determined to showcase the family's notorious work ethic, would be spending the entire evening restoring nineteenth-century farm implements behind the closed door of the basement. Maybe Steve was a fellow junk—sorry: antique—dealer, someone who might opportunistically designate himself in charge of all (female) volunteers at the upcoming cheese and sausage festival. What kind of surname would such a Steve have? Steve McWherter. Steve Timmons. Steve Reeve.

"Violet," her mother said. She closed the silverware drawer with what seemed like too much force. "You'll need to pick up Pete's ashes from the vet's office. Tomorrow after school."

"Okay," Violet said. She hadn't known her mother had made the call to have Pete cremated, though when she thought about it, she realized burial plots for pets were neither common nor affordable, and her mother, who was not sentimental, but not cruel, either, might have had some idea about keeping the ashes in an urn on the mantelpiece or walking out to Pete's favorite spot under the weeping willow tree and scattering them to the wind. Her father, who had always hated Pete, would not participate in any mourning rituals, though he would not object to them, either. Their house was a house ruled by a cold, unspoken consensus; one could neither endorse nor challenge, praise, nor lament, not out loud, at least, and certainly not with any energy.

Violet watched as her mother started down the stairs to the basement. "And I'll leave the credit card for you," her mother said. "So you can pick up some steaks at Ralph's."

"Okay," Violet said. She hated steak.

"Ralph is out sick," said her mother, as she disappeared down the stairs. "Ask for Steve."

The next day during band practice, Violet, suddenly paranoid about a previously unheard of Covid variant, took her trumpet and moved her chair and music stand out into the hallway. The band director had been allowing for additional social distancing measures, though most students were taking advantage of the new protocols by skipping class and merely pretending to practice outdoors. But Violet wanted to make a good impression. The band director thought her *talented*, even sent a note home to her parents saying so, and although her dental recovery made playing anything but slow warm-up exercises almost impossible, she badly wanted to maintain her first chair status, and, more importantly, her idea of herself as so serious and unflappable she might be mistaken for an adult. It was the promise of adulthood—escape—that drove her to most of what she did in life, including joining the marching band in the first place; a scholarship might be in order.

At school, she didn't talk much more than she talked at home. For a long time, she'd had only one friend, Kerry, who liked horses so much everyone called her Mr. Ed. The sad truth was that Kerry, who generally was even less talkative than Violet herself, wanted to communicate only by text or Snapchat. Several months before, Kerry had been forced to move to Fort Worth after her stepdad died of Covid. Even after her departure, Kerry remained Violet's one and only friend, and they seemed to talk just as much—or as little—as they had when Kerry lived in Redwood. Still, Violet felt the sting: Mr. Ed's move had left her without a single person to talk to at Redwood High.

In the hallway, she sent Kerry a text.

I thought I wanted to come back to school. But I was wrong.

Kerry usually took at least ten minutes to reply, but this time she must have been already texting with someone else. *I know what you mean,* she said. *I feel like I'm in an ant farm.*

This was part of the reason why Violet liked Kerry, because she did not mind diminishing herself for the sake of saying something unexpected. *I'm supposed to play my trumpet at the cheese and sausage festival,* Violet wrote. *But I had my wisdom teeth out. TOTAL DISASTER.*

Shit, Kerry said. *How the mighty redwoods have fallen.*

They exchanged a few additional texts, short sentences about classes and classmates too cool to consider friends. Kerry was not in the marching band, but she was in the show choir, even though she didn't know how to sing and had no interest in music. Electives: they didn't always make sense. Long-distance texting with Kerry was more or less the same as texting with Kerry had been when she lived in Redwood, and Violet was glad to have someone, at least, who thought her worthy of communication. She told Kerry about the jar of rocks in the bottom of her mother's bag. *Creepy,* Kerry said. *Your mom's a grape nut.*

Shredded wheat, Violet said back. *Total frosted flake.*

The bell rang, and Violet realized she had failed to practice. "The Star-Spangled Banner" was not an easy song to play, and she knew, even under the best of circumstances, she would struggle with the high notes. With her sore mouth she was doomed for sure. She considered speaking to the band director, but rejected the idea: too much speaking. She knew she'd have no choice but to face the music, literally and figuratively, so that no matter what happened at the cheese and sausage festival she'd have to make a go of it and embrace the great honor of having been chosen to perform. After school, she drove first to the vet's office to pick up Pete's ashes. During the worst of the lockdown, her mother had assigned Violet the task of taking Pete for routine appointments— owners remained in their cars, and everyone wore masks. Now in the aftermath of the pandemic, they'd opened up the lobby as if it were a freewheeling bachelor party.

"I'm here about Pete," Violet said at the front desk. "His body, I mean."

"We don't do bodies." The vet tech, who looked to be just about exactly Violet's age, said this from behind the plexiglass barrier. "Do you want to make an appointment?"

"I've already had an appointment," Violet said. "I mean, my mother did."

"You want another appointment?"

"No."

"Low-Dose Super Pest-Off? Freak-out Leather Liner for Cats? Green-Chew Movable Feast?"

"No."

"You'll have to call for an appointment."

"I don't want an appointment."

"Look, the vet tech said. "I don't think I can help you."

Violet turned. She knew she should explain about Old Pete's ashes, but she was afraid that talking about his death would cause her to burst into tears, and already the vet tech had admonished her, made her feel small. As she walked out the door of the vet's office, she knew this was the way life would be in the adult world: people would deliberately misunderstand her, and her unwillingness to correct them would lead to her repeated and ongoing defeat.

On the way to Ralph's, she decided she would lie to her mother, but not right away, and not out loud. For a couple of days her mother would be so busy removing rust from an ancient anvil or sanding down old dresser drawers she would forget to ask about the ashes. In the meantime, Violet would sneak out the back yard and scoop ashes from the barbecue grill, dump them into a cardboard box, and seal it with mailing tape. Afterwards, she would send her mother a text: *Pete's ashes are in a box. I put the box next to your bag by the front door.*

At Ralph's, the parking lot was empty. Through the front window, she could see that the dining room was deserted, the display case a grave. Violet considered pulling up to the drive-through, considered skipping the steaks altogether, but decided instead to step inside and ask for Steve, just as her mother had instructed her to do. She slung her purse over her shoulder—unlike her mother, she was the owner of several functional, even stylish, handbags—and pushed open the door. Before she stepped inside, a large man wearing a bloody apron pushed a metal cart into her shins.

"Sorry," the man said. "Offal."

Or had he said, "Awful"?

"I'm looking for Steve," Violet said. "About some steaks."

"Steve don't work here no more," the man said. "You'll have to check with Clifton."

Ordinarily, Violet would have said nothing, turned away and departed empty-handed, but something about the way the man had rammed her with his cart had stirred inside her some nameless anger, a call to action. Thinking now of the exchange at vet's office, she found herself filled with a new resolve. She stepped back from the man and pointed at his cart. "I need Steve's phone number," she said. "Immediately."

"Everybody always asking about Steve," the man said. "You'd think he was some kind of celebrity or something."

"Is he?" Violet said. "A celebrity?"

"*Shit*," the man said. "*Celebrity Rehab*."

So that was it, then, her mother had become some kind of meth-head, and there were no "steaks" at all, only Steve and his promise of a quick fix. She wanted to lay eyes on this Steve, to see if he was anything like her own drug-dealing Steve, the first-chair alto saxophone player who was also a fifth-year senior and the captain of the MathCounts team. That Steve had pretended he wanted Violet to be his girl-friend for exactly four days, four days during which Violet—what a fool she had been—had looked at apartment listings and imagined the names of their future children. Turned out he'd only been looking for a mule. Her mother's adult-version, she was sure, was just as rotten or worse.

Violet pulled her mother's credit card from her purse, stepped around the butcher's metal cart, and put the Visa platinum on the high, glass countertop. "I'll take three ribeyes," she said. "And tell Steve my mother is married. To a cop." She paused for a moment, then added, "An *undercover* cop."

Her actual father hated cops and always had, but the butcher—perhaps this was Ralph, himself—would not know the difference. Violet watched as he pulled three leaky brown packages from what she hoped was a refrigerated case behind the counter. He pushed the packages toward her. "On the house," he said. "Like I said, Steve don't work here no more, but I'll give him the message."

Violet reached for the steaks, then stopped herself. She didn't want blood on her hands. "Put them in a bag," she said. "I mean, *please* put them in a bag."

The butcher obliged, and she was on her way. By the time she pulled into the driveway, her mouth was killing her; she knew she'd never be able to eat steak, not even if she cut it into the smallest possible pieces. Her mother wouldn't notice. Her father wouldn't even be there. She sent Kerry a text: *Everything is stupid.* Kerry did not reply.

She put the steaks in the refrigerator and saw the closed door of the basement that meant her mother was pounding and sawing, sanding, and spray-painting, exposing the entire household to noxious fumes, just like Santa's little helper down there—she even *looked* like an elf. When silence returned to the kitchen, Violet could hear the faint sound of the oldies station playing from below: something about heartache and the pursuit of popcorn. Her mother would be dancing now, tapping her foot in rhythm to the crooning of the teen idol. Violet did not like to dance. And in spite of her many years in the marching band, she did not even like music all that much, something that made her feel small and uninspiring. She did like flowers and long had been glad she'd been named after one. In their younger years, her parents must have had an affinity for the natural world. When she was small child, they had seemed free and easy, dancing in the kitchen and spontaneously bursting into song, but sometime around her sixth birthday, they stopped singing and dancing together, and her mother would sing only when she thought she was alone. Nowadays, when they were together, her parents seemed like the sterile, never-trod-upon wall-to-wall carpeting inside the waiting room of a morgue.

"Violet," her mother said, emerging from the basement. "Did you bring in the mail?"

"Yes," Violet said.

"Did you put gas in the car?'

"Yes."

"And did you bring home the steaks?"

"Yes."

"Good," she said. "I imagine Steve must have handed you a second grocery bag?"

"No."

"No?"

"No."

"Okay, then," her mother said. "I imagine I'll have to stop in to Ralph's sometime myself."

"Yes," Violet said, and the evening concluded without dinner, without further mention of Steve, without her father coming home, without her mother even remembering to ask about Old Pete's ashes, and without Violet saying another word.

At school the next morning, all the hallways and classrooms had been decorated with enormous cardboard cutouts: rockets and astronauts, mostly, but also blocks of cheese and sausage links, syringes suggesting renewed wellness in the aftermath of mass vaccination. Violet, carrying her trumpet in its case and struggling under the weight of all the books in her backpack, tried without success to dodge a balloon bouquet listing toward her like an injured animal escaping the human gaze. Members of the boys' basketball team, flexing their muscles for the sake of their cheerleader girlfriends, assembled in the middle of the building, claiming their rightful titles as rulers of the school on the raised, wooden platform everyone called The Moon Landing.

The Moon Landing is full of fakes, Violet texted to Kerry. *Just like always.*

A reliable fifteen minutes passed before Kerry texted back a single word: *gravity.*

In the movies, kids like Violet and Kerry—equestrians and members of the marching band—always emerged in triumph over the cheerleaders and jocks, but reality, Violet knew, was much different: everything would go on in its usual humdrum way, students learning lessons and taking tests, teachers pretending not to notice which kids seemed popular and which did not, everyone growing up in the same steady monotony and suburban splendor, the cool kids hopping on the fast track to becoming energy executives and stay-at-home-moms, the uncool kids going to graduate school to become people plagued by doubt. She could see it all unfolding: the children born out of wedlock, the branding opportunities gone wrong, the home loans and credit card debt. She wanted no part of any of it, and the knowledge that she had no choice but to grow up in a world in which no one, not even people supposedly *in charge*, knew the answers to any questions without first conducting a google search, filled her with a nagging anxiety that made her want to conduct her own google search for "nagging anxiety." She'd always been a good student—a little too good, at times—but lately she kept with her a sad, abiding knowledge her diligence would land with a thud: no one cared what she did, not as long as she stayed out of the way.

When the hour for band practice arrived, Violet did what had done every day since in-person school had resumed and took her trumpet out in the hallway. Once again, she tried to practice the high notes in "The Star Spangled Banner." Her initial plan had been to power through and tighten her embouchure, but her lips felt frozen in place, as if still numb from the novocaine. Finally, she eked out a few wheezing honks, not exactly music to anyone's ears. It sounded like some bizarre, atonal mashup of the Mighty Redwood Rockets Fight song and "Yankee Doodle Dandy." All those patriotic songs sounded the same.

She returned her trumpet to its case and put her head in her hands. Not even despair came easily these days; nothing did. When she tried to feel happy, she felt a blank weight behind her eyes. When she tried to feel sad, she felt only the slow hum of boredom. She'd have to google emotional intelligence. Maybe she could take a diagnostic quiz.

It wasn't that the kids who hung out on The Moon Landing hated Violet—that would have required actual judgment—but they were very particular about who was and who was not allowed on The Moon Landing and when. Before and after school, only those in possession of athletic credentials were allowed, and e-sports didn't count. Golf and wrestling were both fine, as was soccer, but girls' basketball and softball? Definitely not. And someone only in the marching band had better stay far, far away. Every once in a while, a student not involved in particular sports or cheerleading could make her way to the Moon Landing, but only if her parents were either rich, willing to buy alcohol for their underaged children, or both. During school hours, The Moon Landing transformed from clubhouse to classroom, as the school's student population was bursting at the seams, and the trailers they'd set up in the parking lot had recently failed a state inspection. Now, as Violet walked from the band room to her Chemistry classroom, she passed The Moon Landing, where a group of twenty or so sophomores was sitting in a circle and reading aloud from *Paradise Lost*.

Violet texted Kerry: *You ever have to read Milton?*

Kerry did not reply.

That evening at home, her mother said the vet's office had called about Old Pete's ashes. Violet's father was doing another double at the warehouse, and her mother had emerged from the basement only long enough to wash her hands in the kitchen sink. Violet knew she'd end up eating dinner alone.

"You didn't pick up Pete's ashes?" her mother said.

"No."

"Then what was in that box you left by the door?"

"I don't know."

"Do you want to bury Pete's ashes?"

"No."

"Scatter them under the willow tree?"

"No."

"You'll have to prepare dinner," her mother said. "And save a plate for your father."

And then her mother was gone. Sometimes, Violet wished her mother had become an actual hoarder and not just a boring old amateur antique dealer. During the early days of the lockdown, her mother had insisted on forced family togetherness, board games and ball games and brunch. She started knitting again and organized hardware into baby food jars. But as the virus took over and time spread apart, they all retreated to their various corners of the house, and soon enough, both parents decided they were essential workers after all and left Violet to her own devices and the pretense of online education. So many modules to complete, so many timed multiple choice quizzes, so many friendly, animated frogs saying, *ribbit, ribbit, let's learn about another ecosystem.* She'd perfected the art of pretending to pay attention. Once, her Chemistry teacher had taught a Zoom-lesson from the toilet. The lid had been down and his pants pulled up; still, everything had turned terrible all at once.

That night after dinner, her mother went to bed early, and Violet took her place on the sofa. After she was sure her mother was either asleep or absorbed in another televised true crime, she took her mother's canvas bag and dumped the contents on the coffee table. Indeed the jar of rocks was still at the bottom, and the heart-shaped rock bearing Steve's name was still at the bottom of the jar. She rummaged through a drawer in the kitchen until she found a black Sharpie marker. She took the heart-shaped Steve rock and put it in a Ziploc bag and then put the Ziploc bag at the bottom of an empty coffee can, a mountain of all-purpose flour on top of the Ziploc bag, and the whole thing in her backpack. She didn't know what she was going to do with it, but she imagined finding a dumpster downtown or conducting a private burial somewhere in the sticks. She shook the jar of rocks until she found a large, perfectly round rock with a long, flat edge. It was the color of chalk. She uncapped the sharpie marker and wrote: Old Pete. She was pleased with her efforts; how satisfying it was to make perfect, thick, black letters. She restored the Old Pete rock to the mayonnaise jar and the mayonnaise jar to the bottom of her mother's canvas bag. As she dragged the heavy bag back to its place by the front door, she realized there was a name for what she was doing to her mother: crazy-making. And she felt oddly dispassionate about it, like a warm glass of water sitting on a table, never admired and never consumed. What was the point of it all? If someone pulled the rug out from underneath the table that held the warm glass of water, nothing would happen; the water would remain.

The day of the Cheese and Sausage Festival arrived, and Violet's sore mouth had all but healed. At home and at school, she'd been practicing at all hours. That morning, Kerry had sent her a text: *WELCOME BACK TO COVID, MIGHTY REDWOOD ROCKETS.* WELCOME BACK TO DISEASE.

Violet took her trumpet from the instrument room and made her way to The Moon Landing. The railings had been decorated with a strange, homemade garland featuring filmy slices of cafeteria-issued American cheese along with sausage links hot-glued to squares of construction paper cut out to resemble rockets. On a hand-drawn poster, Rocket Steve presided over a plate full of rocket cheese. Students were keeping their social distance, but a palpable anticipation hung in the air: isolation was ending, and the world was back in action.

Violet, alone and anxious, ascended the stairs to the Moon Landing. She was supposed to be the opening act, the cue that meant the sausage vendors were free to enter the all-purpose room and the teachers free to pass out paper plates. She held her trumpet to her chest, sat in the metal folding chair, and adjusted the music stand before her. She was supposed to begin with the national anthem, loud and proud, and then transition to softer "walking-around music," suitable for the casual consumption of cheese and sausage. She put the mouthpiece to her lips. But instead of playing the opening notes to "The Star Spangled Banner," she suddenly had another, better idea; she would play something else instead. The only problem was that she had very few songs memorized: the national anthem, "The Merry Farmer," "For He's a Jolly Good Fellow," and—of course—the Mighty Redwood Rockets Fight Song. Finally, she thought of a memorized passage from a song her father had sung to her mother when Violet was a small child, a song she later learned to play herself for the big finale at the Freshman

Spring Sing. "When You Wore a Tulip, I Wore a Big Red Rose." She put the mouthpiece to her lips and played:

You made life cheery
When you called me dearie,
It was down where the blue grass grows.
Your lips were sweeter than julip
When you wore a tulip
And I wore a big red rose

No one seemed to notice she was not playing "The Star Spangled Banner," and the socially-distanced crowd began to move to the rhythm of the song. The sausage vendor entered from the cafeteria, the teachers passed out paper plates. When she was a child—back when her father sang to her mother—Violet had confused the words "magician" and "musician." Now her big moment had arrived, and, as she played the passage over and over again and lifted her eyes to watch the cheerleaders wave their pompons and the basketball players line up at the cheese table, she suddenly felt like both.

The Shark

No one wants to read about corporate culture—why should they?—but when you hear about what happened at Franklin, Lankford, and Lowe, you'll understand how I ended up in the parking lot of Chuck's Paint 'n' Paper in the middle of the night. It was hot, mid-July in Oklahoma, and I'd started wearing shorts to work instead of my usual tasteful ensemble, "business casual" with a feminine flair. And I did not shave my legs. I'd been working at this particular firm eleven years that January, and I figured I'd earned the right to a little relaxation, especially since my coworkers, including the front office staff, accountants, *and* custodians, all were on vacation that week, and I thought I had the place to myself. I did not anticipate the gang of golfer-lawyers would come back early from their sojourn in St. Andrews, paid for by a secret slush fund called "The Think Bank." The Think Bankers were a thoughtless lot, consumed by equal parts ambition and the all-consuming need for what they called "time to dream."

"Surprise," the Think Bankers said that fateful morning, the day I drove the boss to a two-bit hardware store. "Happy Birthday!"

It was not my birthday. But it was not difficult to act surprised because indeed I was astonished, unsure how they'd managed to get to work without disturbing the silence of the empty parking lot outside. "You got me," I said to my boss. "You old so-and so."

"Katie," he said, "I thought you'd gone to Hawaii."

"It's Kate," I said. "I've changed it to Kate. Katherine if clients are around."

"It's not *your* birthday, is it?" he said. "I mean, this whole thing is supposed to be for Edward's Nifty Fifty."

"Edward's not so nifty," I said. "And he's in Greece."

"He's missing his own surprise party," my boss said. "Not to mention the big game."

"What big game?" I said, a mistake, I realized, the instant the words left my mouth. Wasn't there *always* some kind of big game?

"*What big game?*" My boss said, mocking me. "You're such a kidder, Katie."

An unspoken rule of the twenty-first century workplace dictates you're not allowed to say anything bad about the local sports teams, even and maybe especially if the men in your workplace strategically banter about the latest coach-and-player dog-and-pony-show at the actual or proverbial water cooler as an overt attempt to make themselves feel more at ease and the women less so. They select their favorite sports and favorite teams according to existing regional loyalties, place of origin, and general nostalgia, but also according to temperament. Men who imagine themselves noble usually follow baseball, and the white ones who are nobler still sometimes showcase their tolerance by also following the NBA. I knew it was baseball season, of course, but was unaware of any high stakes jockeying for position in the National League West. Turned out they were talking about a *little league* game featuring that seventeen-year-old left-handed ace—you guessed it—the boss' son. His name was Chase. Chase the Ace. That night, a scout from the Texas Rangers was coming to watch the game.

"You should come with us," he said. "We're sitting behind home plate."

"Not a fan," I said. "And I have to work."

Indeed I could care less about baseball, much less little league baseball, but in my workplace and among my family members both I was an anomaly, a plebeian among pennant-wavers of every stripe. My mother in particular lived and died by teams various and sundried, the more hapless the better. She was one of those women all the men except my father found relaxing and refreshing, a regular den mother, if only she still invited people over and served them mysterious, homemade dips. That summer she was ill, in the hospital, probably going to die. But worse than the cancer was the hospital's bare-bones cable package, a crime against humanity, she said, since she was missing all her favorite programs on ESPN. On top of all that, she seemed to long for a lost era that barely existed in the first place, forever indulging in a foggy fantasy of nurses wearing stiff paper caps and doctors ducking into her room for a secret smoke.

If doctors did such things nowadays they would do them in my mother's room, where she would tell them to take a load off and let them in on the secret behind some offensive coordinator's trick play calling. She knew next season's schedule before anyone else did. She won all the office pools and twice made accurate predictions as to the Super Bowl's final score. For these reasons and several others, I hated sports and all their boring lore.

And of course my boss loved my mother. He visited her in the hospital, gave her balloon bouquets and autographed photos of Chase.

"That's OK," my boss said, after I'd declined attendance at the big game. "Chase will understand. And I get it about not being a fan. Once upon a time, I cared very little for college basketball, for example. But then I realized: in sports, even college basketball, *things are happening*. Live, not tape-delayed. You can't get that anywhere else on television."

"What about reality shows?" I said. "And cooking shows, too. Those people really go on dates. Those people really bake cakes. Sometimes they do both at the same time."

"It's not the same," he said. "I wouldn't cross the street to see Bobby Flay, but I'd watch paint dry if someone was keeping score."

"Score one for the hardware store." I'd meant this as a slight: the boss' daughter, a twenty-one-year-old high school dropout who resembled Joni Mitchell, worked at the local hardware store, Chuck's Paint 'n' Paper. He bragged constantly about Chase's every stride into stardom, but made a point never to talk about his daughter unless it was to complain about the cost of her various medications, none of which, he claimed, she actually needed.

"How's your mom doing?" the boss said. "I meant to email her about her first-round draft picks."

"She's fine," I said. "She's about to die."

"That's cold, Katie," he said. "No wonder they call you The Shark."

I would like to say I earned my nickname from winning high-stakes cases, working eighteen-hour days, seeking blood in the water while the lazy beach bums wasted their lives near the safety of the shore. But the truth was they called me The Shark because my parents, drunk after a World Series win, had given me the unfortunate middle name, "Amity Island." Katherine Amity Island Smith. In addition to their love of sports, they were big Spielberg fans, allegedly because my mother once was his neighbor in Phoenix, Arizona. My brother—Elliot Thomas was his name—distanced himself from their oddities long ago, but some people still called him E.T.

"The Shark has a shitload of work to do," I said. "And I'm merely speaking the truth about my mother. *Trying to prepare myself,* as they say."

"I think they have classes for that," my boss said. "You know, support groups and such."

"I'm glad you attended those sensitivity training sessions," I said. "I'll bet you got an A."

Judging from these comments you might think I was cheeky, irreverent to the point of threatening my own job, but the truth was Franklin, Lankford and Lowe actively encouraged insubordination, even in written documents passed around in meetings, at first as an exercise in encouraging teamwork, and later as a fully institutionalized doctrine describing strategies for disruptive innovation. The result was an office full of tough-talking do-nothings, and I was no exception.

"I'll let you know what the scout says," he said. "You know, after the big game."

Later, at the hospital, my mother slept in fitful bursts while a parade of visitors brought flowers and fruit, neither of which she was allowed to have in her room. The results of her latest blood work demanded a moratorium on beauty or delight, not that the flower arrangements were particularly beautiful or the fruit delightful—more like wilted and bruised—so it became a matter of either sending everything straight to the trashcan or making unwanted offerings to the nurses' station, a walled-off corner where underpaid people in scrubs lurked behind computer screens and slurped from 32-ounce sodas, but rarely walked or talked. I knew you were supposed to suck up to the nurses—and I tried, really I did—but they could tell I was not like them and so pretended not to hear me.

I went downstairs for a cup of coffee, and when I returned, Chase the Ace was in a stiff-backed chair at my mother's bedside, chatting amicably and fiddling with the remote control. They did not see me, not at first, but I could tell he was trying without success to find something very particular on television, doubtless a sporting event of one kind or another, though every channel seemed to show the usual daytime fare: talk shows and cooking demonstrations, jaunty weathermen and lighthearted fake and/or real news. I hid behind the door to her never-used bathroom—she was too weak to get out of bed—and listened to their conversation.

"I don't want to play professionally," Chase said. "But you know. My dad."

"Your dad needs to consider your wishes," my mother said. "Have you tried to tell him?"

"I wish I was gay," he said. "That'd be easier to tell him."

"Are you?" she said. "Gay?"

"No," he said. "I mean, I don't think so."

"Then you should play in the game today. Go warm up that arm."

Her advice was ludicrous, of course; she'd been dispensing this kind of unwanted wisdom since I was a small child. Neighborhood children would stop over for popsicles and leave convinced they should study world religions or demand their parents serve only grapefruit or become fashion designers for dogs. Chase the Ace was a good pitcher—I knew that—and provided he escaped injury he might have been able to get a full scholarship somewhere and come away with some kind of half-assed degree in general studies or sports media, but I failed to see how being gay or not-gay had anything to do with his decision as to whether or not to go pro. I decided to make my presence known.

"Who wants coffee?" I said, pretending for the first time to notice the dancing colors and banal chirps from the television screen. "What's on?"

"Katie," my mother said. "I'm glad you're here. The nurses need their magazine subscriptions renewed."

"What magazines do they get?" Chase said. "Do they have *Muscle and Fitness?*"

"Oh yes," my mother said. "These nurses are muscular. And fit."

"Just saw your dad," I said to Chase. "He mentioned you."

"My dad," Chase said. "is obsessed with me."

I said, "Don't let it go to your head."

"His head is fine," my mother said. "A fine, round head."

We pretended to watch *Wheel of Fortune* for a while, my mother talking over the TV to root for her favorite contestant or praise Pat Sajak's handsome wardrobe. I had an old friend whose father died while he was watching *Wheel of Fortune*, so it occurred to me my mother might die right then and there during the closing credits. I didn't want her to die, but I knew she was going to. More than anything, I wanted Chase to leave.

"The terrible truth," he said, more to my mother than me. "is that I don't really like baseball. What I'd really like to do is to become the big name behind my own start-up. Like some kind of cool app that knows what condiments you want on your burgers before you even place your order."

"There you go," I said. "Dream big."

"Burger Boy," he said. "Burger Town."

But my mother had fallen asleep again, her chest rising and falling more slowly than before. The television played one of the more depressing scenes from *Schindler's List*. Chase, who seemed oblivious both to my attempts to make fun of him and my mother's indifference, continued speaking at a rapid clip. He wanted better furniture, he said, a sectional sofa. And a game room, something big enough for air hockey *and* a pool table. And everyone was into sports cars these days, but what he really wanted was a racing bicycle, the kind you could fold up and put in a suitcase. Under the right circumstances, the Burger App would be just a sideline, something to get him started before he began his career in underwater welding. By then, I had finished my coffee. I crumpled the cup and threw it in the trashcan, loudly.

"Careful," Chase said. "You'll wake up your mom."

I looked at the clock. I didn't know what time the big game was set to begin, but it seemed to me he was running the risk of being late for warm-ups. I looked at the clock again, and then looked at my watch for comparison. The dual scents of bad hospital food and urine wafted in from the hallway. Chase checked his phone and pulled something from his pocket, a small, wrapped package the size of a stone. Turned out it *was* a stone, pilfered from the beach at St. Andrews and meant to bring health and wellbeing to my mother.

"It's a little late for that," I said. I looked at my sleeping mother, her mouth open and her hair stuck to her forehead. She was propped up against four or five pillows at least, but she looked uncomfortable, one shoulder higher than the other, her arm pressed into the bars of the hospital bed. I tried and failed to move her, to place her head more squarely on top of one of the pillows, but she was stiff and bloated, like a weighted balloon.

"Yeah," Chase said. "When she wakes up, make sure to tell her I went to the game."

I promised I would. I waited around for a half hour or so after Chase left, but my mother did not stir. I hated to leave her, but the leave-taking had become a ritual of its own terror and dread: one could never do enough. I hated to leave, but I left her. Every day I arrived, every day I departed. My visits took on a kind of sadness of sameness, the tragedy of the mundane. Often someone else—a man, usually, someone not related to us or even of notable merit in the friendship department—monopolized all her waking hours. She overextended herself making small talk, and by the time the visitor left she was exhausted and fell into an instant state of speechlessness the moment the door closed and left us there alone. I badly wanted to spend the day with her alone, to climb into bed with her like I did when I was a child. But I never did that. Her bed was quite small, for one thing, and I thought it important somehow to keep things light. I told her I loved her a million times but never once did I tell her I would miss her when she was gone. That day, I went back to the office—this time with the place all to myself—to work.

Because the Think Bankers had celebrated Edward's nifty fifty without him, the place was a mess: paper plates with half-eaten pieces of cake littered the reception area, the broken refrigerator was filled with jars of olives and cans of beer, and someone had dumped the contents of a paper recycling bin into a heap on the floor in front of my desk, makeshift confetti I assumed, or a search for documents discarded in error. I took a beer from the fridge and started work on something meaningless and easy, the real reason I was a treasured employee, because of my reliable—and, now that I thought about it, idiotic—willingness to take on all the tasks everyone else found too tedious. The beer made the time go by faster, so I had another, and then another, skipping dinner in favor of a few olives and an ancient package of croutons. At first I lined up the empty beer cans in strict formation on the windowsill, but after a while I stopped counting, allowing some to fall onto the floor and others to tip over on my desk. Amazingly, drunkenness improved my powers of concentration, and I was on a roll. I finished my monthly report and started fabricating numbers for the following month; no one would know the difference, and I'd earn some extra down time as a result. I was about to cash in my chips and call a car to go home when my boss, shaking his head and slurring his speech, met me in the lobby. He, too, was drunk, though his was the kind that seemed to suggest an impending trip to the toilet.

"You want some birthday cake?" I said. "Might make you feel better."

"Katie," he said. "Go home."

"Headed that way now," I said. "Go home yourself."

"Can't," he said. "The game."

I knew this was my cue to ask about the scout from the Rangers, to feign admiration and awe for Chase's next big career move. But it was late, and it seemed to me the game should have been long over. I knew enough about baseball to know there were sometimes extra innings, but it was almost midnight, and though the boss often kept late hours at work, he did not often show up drunk to the office. I generally restricted my own public drinking to holiday parties and expensive outings with important clients, so I did my best to conceal my inebriated state.

"Right, the game," I said. "How *was* the game?"

"I was wrong about the scout," he said. "He's not coming until next week."

I thought we were wrapping things up. But he kept going on about the game, only it wasn't a game of baseball he was talking about but a game of chess, one that had gone tragically wrong. In between gulps and sobs and incoherent searches for his missing cell phone, he explained to me that his delinquent daughter, the one who looked like Joni Mitchell, had spent the evening playing in an underground speed chess tournament in the alleyway behind Chuck's Paint 'n' Paper. And she'd won, too, match after match, until the final round, for the championship. And she'd won that match as well. Everything had been going great, he said, until she went to her boyfriend's apartment to tell him about her victory, and, according to the boyfriend's neighbors who saw the whole thing from their balcony across the street, the boss' daughter and her boyfriend had stood on the front porch and argued, about the boyfriend's knowledge of chess and her long hours at the hardware store, and the boyfriend shot her, shot his daughter, and—here was the part he could not quite choke out—killed her. His daughter was dead. He'd never even told me her name.

"Oh my god," I said. "Oh, no."

"I haven't even told my wife," he said. "The cops called Chase."

"Where is your wife?"

"I don't know," he said. "Somewhere."

"Call her," I said. "Call her now."

"I tried," he said. "Chase tried, too. She won't pick up."

"You have to keep calling," I said. "Did you try texting?"

"I'm not an idiot, Katie."

He and his wife had been embroiled in their own argument, he said, before the big game. They'd been in the drive-through line at a fast food restaurant when a college boy in a pickup truck hit them from behind. The boss had said it was his wife's fault for taking so long looking at the menu, and his wife said it was the college boy's fault for not paying attention, and, though they both had been very hungry, they left without getting anything to eat and didn't even stop to get the college boy's insurance information. "She dropped me off at the game and drove off alone," he said. "Probably went to some kind of pottery class or yoga class or class for people who hate their husbands."

Launching into an uninterrupted chain of inarticulate cries, he said he was sorry for eating too much birthday cake at Edward's nifty fifty, sorry for spending too much money in St. Andrews, sorry for leaving his wife and daughter at home. He was talking non-stop, at times nonsensically, so that his voice rose and fell in robotic bursts, at once operatic and mechanical, both frenzied and hushed. At some point I came to the conclusion I was sober or, at least, sobering up. I knew I should take him either to the hospital, the police station, or his house; it seemed right to help him somehow, only he was too distraught to be cooperative, and I could not interrupt him long enough to decide what should come next.

"I don't even know how she learned to play chess," he said at one point. "Probably she learned from some goddamned lesbian grandmaster in goddamned prison."

"You should go home," I said. "I should take you."

But he would not allow it. He insisted his cell phone was somewhere in the office—perhaps at the bottom of any one of several paper recycling bins—and he would not go anywhere until he found it. Together the two of us dumped all the office paper, plastic, and aluminum in a pile on his desk, opened every filing cabinet drawer, even moved the Xerox machine away from the wall and stacked and restacked the magazines in the lobby, but the missing cell phone was nowhere to be found, and his wife went another two hours before finding out about the death of her own daughter. I brewed a pot of coffee and drank most of it myself. The boss was still sobbing intermittently, at one point using the landline to call various friends of his wife and borrowing my phone to send her yet another unanswered text.

"You know, I was just thinking about your mom," he said. "She really liked Jenna. That was my daughter's name. Jenna. She hated me. My daughter, I mean. But she liked your mom. And your mom liked her."

All this was news to me; I had no idea my mother even had met the boss' daughter, much less shared with her some kind of unexplainable intimacy. After my mom died, I heard from a lot of people like that—old friends and classmates who knew her in ways I did not. For a while, it was nice, to learn of different funny things she'd said or influential actions she'd taken on behalf of some impressionable young adult. But after the novelty wore off, their stories—and, later, their blithe disregard for my inability to move past my own grief—became a burden, and I wanted nothing more to do with these nameless strangers from my mother's past. At that point, in the lobby of Franklin, Lankford, and Lowe, my mother still lived, but only barely, and my boss was not grieving so much as suffering the shock of raw loss. He'd always been erratic, but this was something different, a horrific brew of equal parts shame and guilt, an unwillingness to listen to reason, a wild, uncontrollable sob.

"I have to learn to play chess," he said. "For her sake."

"You don't know how to play chess?"

"I never learned," he said. "So what?"

"It's fine," I said. "No big deal."

"I have to go there," he said. "To Chuck's. To see her play in the tournament."

"Phil," I said. His name was indeed Phil, though I'd never before called him that. Before that moment, in fact, I'd never called him anything at all—not Philip or Phil, not Mr. Archer, not "sir," not Mr. Senior Vice President in Charge of Personal Trusts. At Franklin Lankford and Lowe, the etiquette as to how to refer to one's superiors was unclear at best, and I hadn't wanted to make a mistake. But things were different now that his daughter was dead. "Phil," I said. "She's gone."

"You think I don't know that, Katie? But I've never even *been* to Chuck's Paint 'n' Paper. She's been working there for, like, three years, and I've never even been there."

"You want to go there now? Tonight?"

"Yes," he said. "The boyfriend's in custody. Chase is at the police station."

"Wouldn't you rather go join him? At the police station, I mean? Or maybe your wife has gone home by now."

He finally agreed to go by his own house—it was on the way—to check the driveway for his wife's car and then have me drop him off in the empty parking lot of Chuck's Paint 'n' Paper, which I dutifully did, after insisting he use my phone—one more time—to try his wife. He also checked in with Chase at the police station. We drove mostly in silence. I somehow imagined the alleyway at Chuck's still would be set up for chess, but it was empty, a single streetlight casting a shadow on the grease stains on the pavement below. And though the car's air conditioning was on full-blast, it was hot, and I was suddenly self-conscious about my failure to shave my legs. It occurred to me that the boss and I had never before been in a car together, and something about the sound of cicadas outside seemed strangely intimate, as if we'd been set up on an unsuccessful blind date in some part of a distant, shared mutual past, something like the summer between high school and college, between divorces maybe, post-AA meeting, looking for love in all the wrong places, two middle-aged clichés.

"You want to get out?" I said. "Look around?"

"I thought it would be bigger," he said. "More like Home Depot or Lowe's."

"Where do you think they played chess?"

"By the back door, probably. Where there's enough light to see the board."

I didn't know what to say, so I said nothing, put the car in park and killed the engine. The boss did not make a move for the door. He said he wanted to sit there, just a while longer, to consider the costs of his failure as a father. I thought he was being melodramatic, also perhaps a bit self-centered, since taking an interest in his daughter's chess career or hardware store career or even her entire person probably would not have stopped the boyfriend from doing what he did. But I knew better than to speak at all.

"You do a good job, Katie," he said. "At the firm."

"I know."

"Probably you should be in line for a raise by now."

"Probably."

"Tell your mom I'm sending her some season tickets. Okay?"

"Okay."

We both knew my mother was too weak to use them, probably too out of it to care. I drove him to the police station in silence, and though I knew it would be the right thing to do to attempt to hug him or pat him on the shoulder or at least send my sympathies to Chase, I did none of those things and instead told him to take some time off before coming back to work, as if I were his boss and not the other way around.

In the parking lot of the police station—brighter and cleaner than the parking lot at Chuck's—he took on an official air, suddenly formal and overly polite, stiff and serious in the manner of someone whose actions were being recorded and saved for a court date later on. After he closed the car door behind him and started for the fortress of the police station, I turned off the air conditioning and activated all four power windows, foregoing the radio in favor of the sound of the wind. By then it was practically the middle of the night. I decided to go see my mother.

She might have been asleep, I reasoned, but for once she would be free from other visitors. I could fluff her pillow or refill her water or just take some odd comfort in watching her sleep. And the television. For once, the television and its endless loop of sports highlights and *Jurassic Park* Parts One and Two would be thankfully, wonderfully, most decidedly off.

In the hospital's elevator, I found myself—as always—thinking about work. I wondered how long the boss would be out, whether or not we'd send a delegation to the daughter's funeral, whether the culture at Franklin, Lankford, and Lowe would coarsen or become suddenly soft. In any case, I knew I would forever be missing out on those conversations like Can you believe that politician hugged Jerry Jones? That so many professional athletes have played golf with the president? Can you believe Jim Harbaugh took a pay cut to coach at Michigan? Can you believe we're ranked in the top ten? Can you believe our offense/defense this year? Can you believe the game lasted seventeen hours and forty-two minutes? Can you believe we didn't win? Can you believe we didn't lose? Can you believe your mother has a pressure sore on her tailbone? That she has a tumor the size of a grapefruit at the base of her esophagus? That she still eats? That she still breathes? That for her, worse than the latest CT scan results were the cheapskate administrators making sure the hospital didn't get Fox Sports South? That the Bowl Championship Series changed the rules for the post-season? That the NFL playoffs lasted so damned long? That a concussion could make you smarter? That she lives and breathes? That you're standing there at the door of her hospital room, watching as she calls out for someone to help her, for someone to please god help her, and you're unmoving, like an imagined threadbare set of curtains in a house where no one lives, stuck there with the door open, a crack just wide enough for you to see her struggling with her walker, and in spite of all your constant sadness and desperation and fear of walking this earth alone, you're standing there, afraid to go in?

Paper Fan

Not the object, but the idea for an object, blueprints for an oscillating fan made from the magic of a 3-D printer. "It's my idea," she says at the board meeting. "Don't steal it."

I don't go to board meetings, but my roommate does. She's too young for board meetings, but she doesn't care. Her name is Angelique. Everyone calls her Angel, and I have some idea why. They call me Turkey Lurkey, but my name is Lauren.

Angelique thinks I need to *become more involved in the community.* I think she needs to go jump in a lake. One thing she's heavily involved in is *community advocacy.* She advocates for members of the community. One of the ways she does this is to turn her uncle's lake house into a community center, a safe space, the sign says, for members of the LGBTQ community. Angelique herself has a steady boyfriend who lives in another state. They video chat.

"What are you wearing?" Angelique says into her laptop.

They're sharing a long-distant candlelight dinner—Subway sandwiches—at their respective desks.

"Can't you see what I'm wearing?" her boyfriend replies from the screen.

"No, I mean, what *pants* are you wearing?"

"Oh," he says. "Jeans."

His name is Brett, and he acts like someone named Brett. He wears a lot of jeans.

Angelique and Brett are getting married as soon as he finishes his internship in another state. I'd tell you which state, but it's too boring. I'd tell you what kind of internship, but you can probably guess: a *really important* internship. As our evil president might say, *a very big deal.*

But back to the oscillating fan made from the magic of a 3-D printer. These ideas are *in development.* Angelique is working on a *prototype.* She invented this notion, she says, because we live in Oklahoma, and Oklahoma is very hot. This is *life-saving* technology, she says, *true innovation.*

Angelique has invited me to her uncle's lake house in order to stage an intervention. The lake house is very hot. In the corner, Angelique has positioned an oscillating fan, not one made from the magic of a 3-D printer, but one from Walmart, made in China by people Angelique believes in need of therapy.

"We're intervening," Angelique says from her uncle's leather sofa. "Brett and I think you need help."

"Brett isn't even here," I say. "He lives in another state."

"He lives in a state of awareness," she says. "Hyper aware-ness."

"Sure," I say. "Let's watch TV."

"He's also inside my laptop," she says. "Waiting."

"Waiting for what?"

"Your intervention," she says. "This is your second birthday."

"It's my actual birthday," I say, because it is, not that Angelique—and certainly not Brett—would know.

"Happy Birthday," she says. "Brett and I think you're gay."

"Brett thinks 'salmon' is one of the books of the New Testament."

"Brett doesn't eat fish."

The lake house is suddenly very stuffy. I imagine what Angelique must look like at one of her board meetings, a yellow pencil in her hair made to look messy on purpose. Outside, twilight wraps around the lake. A beautiful purple light streams in from the windows. I hear nothing save the sound of the oscillating fan.

"You're the one who's gay," I say. "And Brett's so super-gay he eats brunch instead of breakfast or dinner."

"Brett likes waffles," she says. "That's all."

"I'm gay enough," I say. "Gay enough to tell you to go jump in your uncle's lake."

"The lake belongs to The People," she says. "It's in a public trust."

"Go jump in the public lake," I say. "Go jump in the *gay* public lake. I'll babysit your oscillating fan."

"You need to face your identity, Lauren," she says. "This isn't funny."

What she doesn't know is that Brett really is gay, or bisexual or mostly straight or mostly gay or maybe just really obnoxious. She doesn't know I've seen him kiss another man.

Not live, but in a YouTube video, and because the other man is on my cousin's basketball team in another state, I know they were lovers in the official sense, for a while. But I don't tell Angelique any of this. She's too angelic to handle it.

"Yeah so I'm gay," I say. "You've successfully intervened."

"I want you to feel safe here," she says. "Really. No one will call you Turkey Lurkey if I can help it."

"Thanks," I say. "That means a lot."

And I'm not lying—not really. Her efforts at outreach—at reaching out—do mean *something*, if not exactly *a lot*. Angelique is the kind of person who needs projects, and I see now I'm one of them. A Science Project: How To Transform Turkey Lurkey Lauren from a Boring Gay Person who never goes out into a Fun Gay Person who Makes Mixed Drinks and Sparkled Sweaters for Rescue Animals. And I don't mind, not really. I consider the merits of becoming a new person, a better person, a person who does not make fun of other people's innovative ideas. I look down at her uncle's coffee table and see a stack of magazines and some unopened mail. On top is a flyer for a local ice cream shop. Angelique turns on the TV, a home decorating show featuring decorators of ambiguous sexuality.

"Turn up the volume," I say. "I can't hear."

When she obeys, I take the ice cream shop flyer from the stack of mail. I fold it, accordion-style, into a paper fan. I fan myself because this is Oklahoma, and I am very hot. I am also very funny, a funny gay person from Oklahoma. Coquettish, I hold the fan so that it covers most of my face. "Look at me now," I say to Angelique. "Ready for the Pride Parade."

"Don't be an idiot," she says. "You're not even on the Steering Committee."

"Steering Committee for what?"

"Pride."

Maybe she *does* know Brett once had a male lover. Maybe the two of them are on the Pride Steering Committee, together. Before I can ask, she grabs the paper fan from my hand and rips it to pieces. "We're allies now," she says. "You can trust me."

"How about Brett?" I say. "Can I trust him-?"

"Brett may be a distant relative of Jared Kushner's," she says. "But don't let that fool you."

"I won't," I say. "You can count on me."

And I mean it, too, because I like Angelique, not because she likes me in return, because she most certainly does not. I like her because she once saved an elderly dog from a burning building and never talks about it. Really. Her mom told me about it. On video chat. "Let's order a pizza," I say. "You think they'll deliver all the way out here?"

"I'm just sure they will," she says. She's loosening up now, grabbing a throw pillow from the sofa and hurling it into my lap. "We're having fun now, Lauren. Aren't we having fun?"

"Speak for yourself," I say. "This gay person," I say, pointing to my own chest. "Doesn't know how to have fun."

"You're so funny, Lauren," she says. "I shouldn't have ripped up your paper fan."

"If only we had a 3-D printer," I say.

"Yes," she says. "If only we did."

Shoobie

Once, a long time ago, I knew a guy named Martin who did not like to be called Marty, though I'd heard another man, Charles, who himself allowed people to call him Chuck, call him Marty on several occasions. So he, Chuck that is, was the only one allowed to call him Marty, perhaps, though I'm not sure, because Martin was afraid of Chuck, or, at the very least, afraid of appearing uptight around Chuck's Mustang convertible and collection of antique golf clubs he kept in the trunk.

"I'm going to bake some pies," Martin said to me one afternoon, late, when the sun slid down the windowpane like so many ripe fruits gone rotten in the fields. Martin and I were coworkers, though saying so implies some kind of cooperation that did not in fact exist. He sold men's shoes, I sold women's, which is to say, I had all the customers and he had all the free time.

"What kind of pies?" I said. I was counting down my

drawer, something I'd learned to do while talking at the same time. Martin was clearing the showroom of loafers and high tops and heels. We were supposed to run the vacuum, but we always skipped that part and cut out early.

"Key lime pies," Martin said, "Chuck's favorite."

"You hang out with Chuck?" I said. This was news to me.

"Chuck's very into Key lime pie," he said. "He wants to move to Florida."

Something to know about Martin is that he loved other men, but was not, to my knowledge, gay. Back then—when I was a mere underling at the shoe store—I myself was gay, or thought I was, but had yet to tell anyone about it. Nowadays I'm still gay, but everyone knows about it and finds it very boring. Who can blame them? I'm the manager of the shoe store now, however, a single step up in the long staircase of life. I don't know what ever became of Martin.

"I thought Chuck didn't like Shoobies," I said. Shoobies was our name for people who'd worked at the shoe store six months or fewer. Chuck was an old hand, having worked there most of his adult life and not once but twice refusing promotion to manager. He said the extra responsibility would interfere with his social life, which, to my knowledge consisted of little more than teaching ballroom dancing lessons and attending the occasional *Star Trek* convention. Still, Chuck was popular. Martin, in particular, loved him.

"You're right," Martin said. By now we'd locked up for the night and had decided, after some deliberation, to have a smoke in the parking lot before going home. "Chuck *does* hate Shoobies, but he's made an exception for me."

"You're like Chuck's Special Shoobie, then?"

"What's that supposed to mean?"

"Just that you two are buddies, that's all. Like the two of us."

"Not like the two of us," Martin said. "Nothing like the two of us."

"Does Chuck like coffee?" I said. "Because coffee goes well with pie."

"I don't think he likes coffee," Martin said. "Look, can we stop talking about Chuck?"

"You're the one who always wants to talk about Chuck," I said. "Shoobie."

When I realized our relaxed parking lot chat was turning into a fight, I decided to pull the plug and go home. Besides, I had to be at work early the next day. After Martin hoisted himself up into the cab of his truck and was safely around the corner, I went back into the shoe store to check the schedule; I wanted to know if either Martin—or Chuck—was assigned to my same shift the following day. To my relief, they both had the entire day off and I instead would be working with a woman named Michelle, who was several years my senior and a very hard worker, if a bit aloof. All that would have been fine were it not for my increasingly obsessive thoughts about Martin and Chuck. All the next day, while I sorted and stacked Hush Puppies, while I stretched slipper socks onto the callused feet of churchgoers, while I cut my middle finger on a pair of girls'-sized soccer cleats, my mind wandered to what Martin and Chuck must have been doing without me: listening to old ballroom dancing tapes while riding around in Chuck's Mustang convertible, touring our town's finest golf courses, eating slim and glistening slices of Key lime pie. It was then I realized the imagination was more powerful than actual experience, and began what became a lifelong interest in metallurgy and handcrafted jewelry. To this day, I sell ankle bracelets under the table in the back room of the shoe store.

About a week later, Martin, who by that time had officially changed his nametag so that is said, "Marty," stopped into to the store one night when he wasn't working, though he was still wearing his stupid nametag, a habit, he said, besides he wasn't entirely at ease in his civilian attire. I thought at first he'd stopped in to pick up his paycheck, but when I looked on the shelf where the paychecks usually were—this was before the days of widespread automatic electronic deposit—I saw only a layer of dust and the same dull pencils with chewed-up erasers that were always there, a mark of our then-manager's untidy habits, though I've long since removed the offending shelf and replaced it with a digital clock.

"Hey, Marty," I said. "Where's Chuck?"

"It's Martin," he said. "Pay no attention to the name tag."

"You and Chuck out on the town?" I said. "Gone golfing?"

"Chuck's getting married," he said, his voice unsteady, like the rhythm of an old rocking chair when it rocks, for a while, even after the person who was sitting in it has risen to his feet.

"Chuck would never get married," I said, even though I'd never before heard the details of Chuck's personal life. "Say, Marty. Martin. Why are you crying?"

"It's because of you," he said. He put his finger to my chest and pressed, hard. "I'm crying because of you."

The Quisenberry
Family Singers

The mayor, knee deep in a muddy creek, thought his vacation a success. He pulled up his boots and waded toward the opposite bank. A catfish, puckered and heavy with age, wriggled in his net. Poison filled the gills of sea life far and wide, and the mayor knew better than to expect a worthy dinner from his efforts. In any case, the idea of slicing into the fish's belly made him sick. Rarely did he manage to catch anything. He didn't even have a boat. When he dumped the catfish back into the water, mud splattered his eyeglasses. He couldn't see. The rest happened so fast he barely had time to clean the lenses on the tail of his shirt.

"I have what you're missing," said a voice from the shore.

"Hello?" said the mayor.

"You heard me," said the voice. "Put your fears to rest and give me twenty dollars."

The mayor replaced his glasses and looked out through the muddy fog. Here we shall encounter a vagrant, he supposed. In the old days we might have said hobo. The word homeless, he knew, faded from fashionable and charitable discourse long ago. What was the appropriate term? Downtrodden? Dispossessed?

"I can't help you," said the mayor, still unsure where to direct his reply. He reeled in his line and moved for the dock. "I don't need your help," said the voice. "You need mine."

The mayor needed help, all right. Every fourth of July he undertook his solitary fishing expedition for the same reason a traffic cop might blow a whistle: to keep the civic peace. The entire first family left town. His wife made her annual pilgrimage to a horse and rider luxury spa in another state. The mayor understood his money was paying for all the family horses to eat grass and stand in the sun while teenaged members of the barn staff braided their tails and polished their hooves. The riders—all women—relaxed indoors with manicurists and massage therapists. Meanwhile, their two younger daughters stayed with the mayor's mother in the city. Their oldest daughter, the great Harvard success story, never came home. Doubtless all the residents of Market Town used the first family's absence as an excuse to gyrate with patriotic glee.

The mayor looked around for some sign of his antagonist— a rustle in the bushes or pebbles dropping in the creek. Mulberry branches swayed in the wind. Finally, a man wearing a tuxedo emerged from behind a magnolia tree.

"Look, I don't want to buy anything and I already have a ticket for the play," the mayor said, reaching for his tackle box on the dock. The Waterville Wilderness Retreat Center rolled out the red carpets for a dinner theater on the first Saturday of every month, even the fourth of July. The mayor, who played Hamlet in college and once tried to start a symphony orchestra in Market Town, never missed a show.

As the man came closer, the mayor recognized him as one of a small, regular crowd who attended meetings of the Market Town Board of Education. Considerably younger than the mayor, the man reached up and scratched a head that seemed too large for its body. He might have been in a commercial for dandruff shampoo. His features, a thick neck and smooth jaw, were like those of a professional baseball player. The mayor thought he might be a Mormon.

"Your car keys," the man said. "You dropped them in the lodge. I didn't mean to scare you, Mr. Mayor."

Fine way to greet a man, the mayor thought. How dare this cretin interrupt his vacation. His one chance for peace and quiet and he found himself followed out of town by the head of the brute squad. For twenty dollars he might kick him in the shins.

"I was just kidding about the twenty dollars," the man said, reaching out his hand for a shake. "Brent Quisenberry. My son's in school with your daughter. Quinn Quisenberry? I think they were in the same homeroom."

"Of course," the mayor said, though he had no recollection of ever having met the boy, or any of his daughter's classmates, for that matter, since he made a point to keep his distance whenever she had friends over to the house.

"Well, it's difficult to make your mark as an eighth grader. The A-honor roll doesn't get you very far in terms of business opportunities. But Quinn's a real punch in the gut, if you know what I mean. A real go-getter. You will hear from him, Mr. Mayor. Before long he'll be too old to keep breaking hearts at the skating rink."

The mayor closed the lid on the tackle box and slung his net over his shoulder. His muddy pants, though a nice change of pace from his usual, more formal attire, embarrassed him. He wanted a hot shower, a nap in the air-conditioned bliss of his private cabin, and a quiet evening at the theater. He wondered why Quisenberry hadn't stuck around for Market Town's celebration of American muscle flexing. The garish display of yellow ribbons and stuffed George Washington heads seemed right up his alley. He finally shook Quisenberry's hand. Overhead, a hawk wavered and dipped. The afternoon sun made a sticky glaze on the back of the mayor's neck as the two men made the short trek back to the lodge. Quisenberry said nothing about returning the mayor's car keys.

"Well, I'm off," said the mayor when they reached a row of picnic tables by the edge of the great hall. Children and their mothers gathered around an enormous poster advertising the upcoming summer theater season. Bricks inscribed with the names of major donors covered the sidewalk leading up to the front door. The mayor blocked Quisenberry's entrance into the lobby and stood with his feet far apart, his shoulders square in the manner of security guards protecting the post office vault. Now assuming his most fearsome pose, the mayor cleared his throat and held out his open hand.

"Guess I'll see you at the show tonight, then. Brought the whole family along, I suppose."

"Oh, we're not watching the show, Mr. Mayor. We *are* the show. Quisenberry Family Singers? The opening act, anyway."

The mayor felt wounded. Earlier he had paid thirty-three dollars for a fourth row seat to *The Three Sisters*. An opening act seemed all too reminiscent of cheap backyard variety shows, of rhinestone-clad fortunetellers at the county fair, of box socials, hillbillies, hay bales, of Market Town itself, the metropolis he governed with simultaneous dread and regret. Here in Waterville, he expected bistros instead of Market Town's many drive-thru McDonalds's. Waterville boasted two art galleries for every gas station in Market Town. And even better, Waterville allowed the mayor the rare opportunity to enjoy a guilt-free evening, a night on the town free from the roaming eyes of the family values crowd. In Market Town, the appearance of every police officer and pothole made him feel depressed. And while Market Town's city manager, a younger, more aggressive man, carried out all the actual administrative duties and possessed most of the meaningful authority, the mayor took his ribbon cutting and ground breaking responsibilities very seriously. His general good health and demeanor signaled prosperity for Market Town, but lately, the ill will of the citizenry left him alone with melancholy thoughts of his legacy: a failed re-election bid, more frequent retreats to Waterville, and a broken down high school gymnasium named in his honor.

"Mr. Mayor," Brent Quisenberry said. "I would be honored if you would join us on stage for the Pledge of Allegiance."

"Yes," said the mayor. "Of course."

Before dressing for the theater, the mayor dialed his home phone number. No one would answer, of course, but he had read about thieves entering the empty houses of wealthy citizens, snatching handfuls of money and jewelry, and displaying the phone book, the phone number for local police circled in red magic marker, open on the kitchen table. The clever burglar then would leave a taunting note scrawled in the margin. *Call this number. You have just been robbed.* Maybe these same criminals would answer the phone when he called. Or maybe his wife, tired of eating health food from wooden bowls shaped like barnyard animals, had packed the horses into their gooseneck trailer and come home early.

"Hello," said his youngest daughter. "Dad?" Caller ID must have given him away.

"Katherine?" the mayor said. "Where's Grandma?"

"Asleep in the front seat of the car."

"Is she all right?" said the mayor, remembering his mother always took naps in the passenger seat of her Toyota. Better to keep an eye on the neighborhood, she said.

"Are you all right?" he said. "Why aren't you in the city?"

"Fine," Katherine said. "We're home for the fourth. We thought we could go to the parade this year. Since you're gone and everything. No offense."

The mayor did not take offense. He knew the residents of Market Town could not stomach his presence on the nation's birthday. Through no fault of his own, he became persona non grata during holidays of symbolic national importance. One year, when Katherine was small, the mayor displayed the Canadian flag on the flagpole at City Hall—a protest, he said, designed to draw attention to America's skyrocketing healthcare costs. After a rally in the mayor's front yard and about a thousand letters to the editor, the controversy died and the mayor promised from that moment forward he would pay proper respect to the memory of the founding fathers. Now he just left town.

"Listen Katherine," said the mayor. He could hear the televised drone of fake laughter in the background. When they were home, he and his wife allowed neither daughter more than a half hour of the highest quality programming. Like everyone else in Market Town, they were making the most of his absence. "Do you know anybody named Quinn Quisenberry?"

"Oh yeah, sure," Katherine said. "All the girls at school call him Quinn Quisenberry, MR."

"You mean they call him Mr. Quinn Quisenberry?"

"No."

"Is this some kind of mean thing about retarded people?"

"No," she said. "Not this time. It's kind of like MD, for medical doctor."

"What does MR stand for?"

A pause, then Katherine said, "I don't know if it's true or not, but they call him Quinn Quisenberry, Marauding Rapist."

This was sobering news. The mayor did not know they had rapists in the eighth grade. Katherine, busy with girl's basketball and French horn lessons, seemed not to know any boys at all. Her mother, the mayor's wife, confessed to the mayor she often worried both daughters were maladjusted, awkward, the kinds of girls who would go their whole lives without receiving invitations to school dances. To the mayor they still seemed like children.

"Stay away from this male rapist, do you hear me."

"Whatever, Dad," she said. "He's not in my crowd."

"I'm serious," he said. "Someone needs to know about this."

"Everybody knows about it."

"And they're not doing anything?"

"You do something," she said. "You're the mayor."

"Go wake up Grandma."

The mayor spoke briefly to his mother and to his other daughter. He dialed his wife and ended up with her voice mail. *Brevity is the soul of wit, so let's get witty: hi honey. How are the horses? I didn't catch any fish. I think we should send Katherine and Karen to private school. Call me.*

Everyone's gone crazy, the mayor decided while shaving. He remembered a time when political change generally worked in his favor. What a dope he had been to imagine the world was getting better. These days all the Market Town manhole covers seemed to open on the command of some malefactor somewhere. Presto, and the sewers rose up into the streets. Change-O, and morality meant mandatory computer time, downloading, dreaming up nicknames for stars of serial dramas, pushing fashionable baby strollers, celebrating the crucifixion over and over again. And for the most part, the mayor, afraid to rock the boat, let the waves of the second millenium's Great Awakening wash over him and drown his better self. He dried his face with a hand towel. A sticker on the bathroom mirror said *Have you heard of the Independence Day special? Non-alcoholic Hurricane. Very good!*

The mayor, dressed in his best suit and newly polished shoes, arrived early for the dinner theater. Platters of Cajun catfish stood waiting under a long line of heat lamps. The mayor ordered water and watched all six of the Quisenberry family singers warm up on stage. The youngest, blonde and boisterous in ruffled underpants, blew recklessly on a pitch pipe. The elder Quisenberry and his wife checked their collective appearance in a compact mirror. The boys adjusted their ties. Set pieces for *The Three Sisters*, trees and a wooden trellis, lurked in the shadows backstage. A piano player begged for the children's attention. Finally, they sang through a couple of numbers from *South Pacific*. A waiter asked the mayor if he would care for a trip to the buffet.

"No thanks," he said. "I'm not hungry."

The mayor tried in vain to hide behind his menu, but Brent Quisenberry, quick like a running back, spotted him from the stage. He bounded down the stairs and jogged buoyantly to the mayor's table. On stage, the piano went silent.

"My car keys," the mayor said. "I've been meaning to ask you."

"Right here," said Quisenberry, patting his breast pocket. "We're all set for the pledge?"

"I've been thinking I just want to enjoy the show."

But Quisenberry wouldn't hear of his family appearing on stage on the Fourth of July without the official public blessing of the mayor.

"But I'm the mayor of Market Town," the mayor said. "Maybe the Waterville people should help you out. How about those car keys?"

"Oh, no you don't," said Quisenberry. "You think you'll just take the money and run, do you? You have a responsibility, Mr. Mayor. You promised."

Right then, the mayor realized his day was done. People like Quisenberry, no longer afraid of their own fanaticism, stood ready to take over the dinner theater, Waterville proper, the lakes and rivers beyond. The Quisenberry brand of progress blindsided the mayor. Before he could gather his resources and prepare for the worst, younger families moved in and claimed a monopoly on virtue. One day he had been walking along Market Town's Main Street, feeling fine, thinking he might stop in to Market Town Morning Coffee for a loaf of bread to bring home for dinner, and before he knew what was happening, the silent majority had become very vocal indeed. Don't buy that bread, they told him. The flour comes from the by-products of stem-cell research. We need to send a clear message to congress.

The clear message, that the mayor and his kind belonged to another era, made him fear for his daughters. A son might swagger through life with the confidence of a soldier returning from war. His oldest daughter, arriving at adulthood just in time to escape the dissonance of the Quisenberry family dance tunes, would manage just fine. The other two, accidents resulting from failed birth control initiatives, arrived too late. Surely they would come under the collective spell of an aggressive band of nationwide monstrous male activists and their female supporters. Nothing could save them.

By now the theater overflowed with hungry patrons. Waterville's finest, their hands clutching at forks and goblets, spoke to one another with boundless energy. The mayor checked his watch. At home in Market Town, the candlelight parade was just getting started. He thought of his mother, fresh from her nap, ordering Katherine and Karen to draw moustaches on the stuffed George Washington heads lining the street in front of their house. Suddenly he longed for the old-fashioned simplicity of Market Town's Fourth of July. Without the mayor's blessing or approval, Waterville now threatened to surpass Market Town in its march toward nationalistic self-destruction.

Just as the curtain was about to rise on the set of *The Three Sisters*, Quisenberry motioned for one of his sons to give up his metal folding chair for the benefit of their important patriotic guest. The mayor found himself face to face with the notorious eighth grade criminal. A slightly smaller version of his father, Quinn Quisenberry rose from his chair.

The mayor said, "I'll stand."

"Suit yourself," Junior Quisenberry said, and as the mayor stood facing the audience, his coat and tie rigid against his skin, he thought himself separate from his city, separate from his family, separate from the theater-goers of Waterville and the parade-watchers in Market Town.

He put his hand on Quinn Quisenberry's shoulder and squeezed, hard.

"You a Chekhov fan?"

"Who me?" Quinn said. "Oh yeah, I like all that stuff. Have you read *The Purpose-Driven Life*?"

"No," the mayor said. "Never heard of it."

"Well you should check it out sometime."

The mayor took his hand from Quinn's shoulder, turned to the elder Quisenberry, and said, "Let's cut to the chase. What's the bare minimum I have to do to get my car keys back."

"The pledge," the elder Quisenberry said. "And when you get to the part that says, *under God*, I want you to do more than just mouth the words."

"I believe in God."

On the edge of the stage, the artistic director wrapped up his pre-show remarks. The mayor, still unsure of his course of action, stepped up to the microphone. He looked out at the crowd.

"How was the catfish?"

No one answered. Finally, a low voice from the front row said, "Shitty!"

Now everyone laughed, and the mayor felt at ease. He caught Quisenberry's eye and a mutual menace passed between the two. Quisenberry patted his breast pocket, indicating the mayor's still missing car keys. At this point, he knew he would never get them back. His political life was over. No more bids for re-election. No more fundraisers or rope lines or phone banks. He could say anything he pleased.

"I know you all like music," he said to the crowd. "And you all love your country. Your God. No one loves his country more or prays to his God more often than Brent Quisenberry, the leader of our next act. So please, put your hands together and join me in welcoming the one and only sign of the apocalypse, The Quisenberry Family Singers."

The mayor turned to Quinn Quisenberry and tried to shake his hand, but the young automaton kept his own hands rooted in the depths of his pockets. The mayor watched as Quisenberry walked past his wife, skirted around the piano, and pointed to the flag hanging from the ceiling. Quinn Quisenberry's baritone voice launched into "America the Beautiful." Without a word, the mayor returned to his seat.

On his plate were steamed vegetables, a baked potato, and Cajun Catfish.

He sliced into the fish's belly. In Market Town, the parade would be over by now. Fireworks would bounce off the stadium walls. His two daughters, alone with their grandmother on the fifty-yard line, would be covering their ears. Here in Waterville, the program continued, the merry notes of the piano ringing throughout the great hall. The mayor poised a dime-sized piece of catfish on the edge of his fork, and, when no one was looking, took a bite.

Just Saying Hello

Bonnie and Ray were retired, though Ray took a side job selling small appliances at Sears, and Bonnie, though she'd worked at the public library for thirty years and was pretty well sick of the place, continued to work Saturday mornings doing story hour for the kids. Ray was at Sears one day when Bonnie decided to get in some exercise and take her bicycle for a spin out in the neighborhood, the "gayborhood," they called it these days, since all the same-sexers had moved in. They were fine people, really fine people, except for Davey and Jonas who had no children but greyhounds instead. Jonas, the younger one—she thought he was some kind of graduate student—was tolerable, friendly in a generic sort of way, but Davey, who worked in finance and made sure everyone knew it, was a creep. And they allowed their greyhounds to shit in everyone's front yard, and no one, not even Ray, who was ordinarily both bold and diplomatic, had the guts to confront Jonas and especially not Davey about the dinosaur-sized turds. The greyhounds were named Rebel and Saint, which Bonnie thought was stupid. Her own dogs, before they died, had been named Peaches and Harley, not perfect names, to be sure, but better than average. On her bicycle now, she saw Davey practicing his golf swing in his front yard. The big decision: to wave or not to wave. At the last minute, she thought of Ray working overtime at Sears so as to have extra money for their winter trip to Florida, and something about the vision of the white sands before her made her decide to go ahead and wave, but she immediately regretted it when Davey, though he was looking right at her, did not wave back.

Birth Certificate

Starting with the first photo, you can expect a lifetime of daffodils wilting, leather and paper, stitches and glue. Expect baptism, window replacement, cold drinks in an ice chest after the last big game. You're starring as an envelope in your school play, the Saturday matinee sponsored by the United States Postal Service, only they won't pay for props. You can borrow or steal, pay discount rates at the Goodwill store downtown, security cameras pointed at the alleyway, pavement pummeled by hailstones the size of your fist. In the gymnasium, tasseled banners bound down from the ceiling, rat-chewed champions still favored first in line at the bank and bed and breakfast, no tomatoes, please. Expect to hear tape-recorded trumpets on Veteran's Day, hip-replacement day, the day the first body comes home in a bag. Say you're not athletic, knees like trailer hitches, artery walls made of mud. All the worse for you. (This is why you were cast as the envelope and not the jolly postman, not the bill for power and light, not the telephone operator, not the master of ceremonies, not the ice cube, not the glass of lemonade). How many haircuts in a lifetime? Be brave and say "none" or "one." Watch yourself step onto the high wire, low by circus standards, still wide enough for the wind. Whitman asked, *are you the president?* You're white, so you dream yourself dancing in the west wing of the White House, the black man reading Whitman and saying *yes.* Poolside, you name your dog Chewy Lewis and pay with a credit card to have his skin shampooed, eyes pink around the edges, breath smelling of disease. Expect to be good. Expect to spend at least one birthday surrounded by nothing save the sound of your own voice. Expect to memorize the quadratic formula, forget which pants have pockets and which do not, join clubs meant to take your money, let them have the money, forget about it, and move on. If you plan for retirement, plan for garden condominiums, energy efficient appliances, spills and divots, rotting tiled flooring, finger foods flavored by your own you-know-what, a porch so small you call it your yard. If your books are overdue, your ceiling cracked, car won't start, neighbors gone to save souls in Cambodia, you're living pretty and you deserve it, yes you do, you deserve every Tom, Dick and Mary to shake your hand, hello there, how's the wife and kids, haven't seen you at the funeral home lately, keeping busy, baby, did you know my Debbie had a baby, oh yes the cupcakes lined up like little dolls, a margarita maker, not for the kids, ha ha, my property taxes gone sky high, what's happening to this country, a farmer boy from around here made it on to that YouTube, lose your shirt, lose your service, lose your life, my how your fingernails have grown.

Hospital Chart

Without the watchful eyes of visitors, a woman drinks tea after surgery. Whether it's hot tea or iced tea depends on geography, backwoods or front of house, packets of ketchup, moist towelettes. In any case, she's thirsty, teeth and tongue like headstones, throat closed like a wooden gate slung on top of a trash heap. She's read about the fifty ways health care reform will help women, number one, she thinks, pregnancy: a permanent state. Number two: too many chicken pox to count. The other forty-eight will have to wait, as she's drinking tea—a "spot," as they used to say, and as she said today, to nurses who thought she meant a stain on the sheets. If she's had something removed from her body, they keep it in a jar. If she's had something added to her body, stitches, say, or a stent, she herself is the jar, pinholes pricked in the lid so captive grasshoppers half-dead at the bottom can breathe. Every day, a surgeon stabs someone and doesn't go to jail. Every night, a woman walks the street and does.

Tea on a tray comes with a lemon wedge, withered where the fruit company's ink smudged the rind, seed-scattered saucer, lumps of old sugar, a pint of frozen milk. One sip and she's convinced of her own greatness, each cell inside her starved for more air. Parachutes, coffee cans lush with lantana, magic tricks, a picture postcard showing starvation victims scaling the Eiffel Tower, teacups stacked to the ceiling: all for her. She knows only two kinds of gowns—evening gown and hospital gown, both open at the back. She vows one day to wear the former, in the evening, far away from the roadside cabin where she stirs wooden pots of paint, the fireplace whispering doom to the broken grandfather clock, stunned silence for the joyless keeper of the hearth. Prisoners are allowed to lift weights. School children spend entire days outdoors, launching model rockets, rocking back and forth on their haunches, rolling eggs along the ground with a spoon. The British say *in hospital* instead of in *the* hospital, just as they go on holiday to Morocco instead of vacation to Duluth. But poinsettias are poisonous to dogs, mistletoe a menace to all but the kissers. She's never worn a tennis bracelet, not to be confused with a sweatband. Too showy, she says, though her daughters wear frayed friendship bracelets to celebrate the cruelties of the seventh grade. Today, her bracelet says only her name, so strange after surgery it seems to belong to someone else, as in movies where the heiress discovers she's an orphan, the loud speaker announcing her ancestry, a crowd of carnival-goers dressed in breezy whites, the fence posts festooned with flowers, the microphone shoved in her face, and her own surprise when her voice sounds more muscular than musical, less lavender than stone.

Ballot

State Question 722 asks voters to consider a century-long prohibition on the use of Sharia law in the judicial branch of the state of Oklahoma. State Question 761 asks voters to consider whether or not Californians ought to have legal marijuana. State Question 777 asks voters to consider preventing Microsoft Word from recognizing the correct spelling of the word "Sharia." State Question 801 asks voters to consider the future of all state questions, whether the necessary steps toward placing a state question on the ballot ought to be made easier or more difficult. In the summertime, the leaves are soft and supple when they fall, early, as if by accident. And when you in your yard see a slice of green velvet floating from its branch, you have several options: leave it be, the wind will sweep it away. Rake it into a pile so small the grass blades dwarf the results. Bend down and let it rest on your finger, the maiden at the wishing well with a butterfly's wing. Bring it inside and put it under your pillow, reach for it in the middle of the night and flatten it on the kitchen table, a dew drop in the light from the refrigerator door left ajar, on purpose, so as not to wake the birds in their cages. Write on it, with a paperclip bent into a stylus, a tally mark for every day spent in the company of strangers. Clean the gutters, wipe the windows in the morning, blow dust from the furnace, soak lentils in a bowl, blanket the horses, harvest the hyacinth bean, scrub the stones free of bruises, save the green tomatoes from frost. Take the bus instead of your bike. Plan for November, that fateful day at the polling place, a church the size of a football stadium, the home of the Oklahoma Chinese Baptist Coalition, pencil poised above the names of every tax-and-spend entitlement program elitist enemy to small business bloated government handout throw the bums out scout for the reds except they're not red anymore I forget what color they are but they're not red white and blue that's for sure, they're brown. Like leaves on trees and the nuts on the ground, dead animals, all of them shriveled from lack of rain.

Book Report

From the beginning of time, man has worried over the state of his wallet, money clip, brown paper envelope, safety deposit box, etc. Nicholas Kleeger addresses these concerns in his classic modern novel, *Fast Free Delivery*. Have you ever gone to a store and found yourself without enough money to buy something special? If so, you can relate to this universal book. We all have had that one unique experience that compels us to sit down at our home computers and write down the longings of the human heart. Nicholas Kleeger longs for vacation time, a shorter commute, a friendlier boss, a new three-piece suit, a cocktail shaker that doesn't leak on his countertop, and, of course, love. If you have ever broken up with your boyfriend or girlfriend, then you can relate to this book for all ages. One day while he's reading the newspaper, a woman carrying two umbrellas (even though it's not raining) tries to talk to him about a mysterious game of Scrabble that takes place every night in the basement of a bar. This is what starts him on his adventure to find love. Most people don't think they can find love at the same time they're trying to play Scrabble, but Nicholas Kleeger thinks he has to write a whole novel about stuff like putting a penny on the railroad tracks, washing your car with the garden hose and being all surprised when the water that comes out is sort of brown and has particles in it, dressing up in a giant hotdog suit and passing out fliers—that part was actually funny—and jogging, I mean this guy does a lot of jogging, like more jogging than they do on the track team, and also looking for his girlfriend at the pound, even though she calls it an animal control facility and he thinks that's stupid, he still looks for her there and goes crazy when he gets locked in a cage and starts thinking about his job and all the trips he has to take, even though the company pays for them. Overall I thought this was a classical book people will read for many years to come. But I wonder why he must make so many complaints when he has a job and a girlfriend and even though his dog ends up in the pound he seems like he doesn't care, which leads the reader to conclude he ought to get counseling for his unhappiness problem, a problem we have all faced in our daily lives, but we don't complain about it half as much as this guy, which is why I recommend this book for people who like big words and sadness, birthday parties for dogs, weird jobs, and people so full of dread they can't face simple tasks like getting up in the morning, their heads throbbing, their wallets empty, houses fallen into disrepair, and the inevitable pain that comes when large appetites are reduced to something small.

April Fool's Day

Girls who grew up in my hometown all became piano teachers or librarians or nothing at all. Of those three I would have chosen librarian, though I liked loud noises and disliked the mass migration from typeface to cyberspace, only just beginning in my public high school with the advent of friendly programs nicknamed "PETE" and "RIGHT-WRITER" meant to teach slow-loading geometry lessons or create the outline of a butterfly on a dot matrix printer. To the miracle of the microchip I made indignant objection on the grounds our souls were starving and machines were the culprits, as if anyone had tears left to shed over the disappearance of phone booths, PVC replacing lead, or children playing with tiny toy machine guns instead of wooden blocks. Really, no one cared. And why should they? Change happens, and people die.

I can't stop feeling bad about progress, though. The other day, a man I know at work made feverish talk about nanotechnology. Young people, he said, stand poised on the verge of a revolution. I tried to say something vaguely insulting—like *heh, heh, yeah, a money-making revolution,* but he just looked disappointed. And yesterday, I had some problems with a digital wristwatch. The sleek, black casing holds the secrets to everything from my resting heart rate to the number of calories in three ounces of chicken, but guess what, the damn thing won't tell time. In the morning, I went out jogging only to look down at my wrist and see 7:53 flashing over and over again. Frustrated, I ripped at the Velcro strap, threw the watch on the hard pavement below, and never looked back. These days, people have abandoned wristwatches, preferring instead to check the time inside the small window to the universe on the face of every phone. Yesterday, after destroying the wristwatch, I crushed my cell phone with a forty-pound dumbbell at the gym. Also, I took a baseball bat to a secondhand laptop belonging to the state of Oklahoma. I'll tell you about it later.

In my youth, I feared authority and refrained from destroying public property. I did cut down a tree, once. Actually, my elderly neighbor cut down the tree while I stood there watching, ashamed. We loaded the branches into the back of his pickup and drove to the dump.

"We're going to get caught," I said. "That tree was on school grounds."

"Enough with the guilt trips," he said. He was wearing a three-piece suit, though he'd taken off the jacket to cut down the tree. His tie was loose around his neck, his sleeves rolled to the elbows. I thought he resembled photos I had seen of FDR—without the wheelchair, of course.

"They'll know you did it," I said. "No one else gives a damn."

"Language," he said.

"You're not worried?" I said. "You don't think they'll come after you?"

"This tree belongs to me," he said. "Even if I killed it, at least it's mine."

"Great logic," I said. "The logic of murderers. The logic of war-mongers. The logic of thieves."

"You've been watching too much CNN."

"Speak for yourself, Mr. Scud-Stud. You're the one with blood on your hands."

Every night I recorded hours of news coverage of the Gulf War on my family's VCR. At school, I led a walk-out protest and passed out black arm bands. Only six of us participated. That night, with my neighbor and the now-dead tree, I thought myself utterly sincere, and good. But I was also afraid.

"You know, Maxine," he said. "You're the most cynical person I know."

I considered myself more worldly than cynical, though I didn't mind the idea I had become wise beyond my years. That I spent much of my leisure time with people older than my parents turned me into a kind of woman-child, not exactly precocious, but weird, nonetheless. Every day after school, I brought the video tapes of the Gulf War coverage over to Hanson's house and we sat there in the green light of his living room, eating granola bars and watching smart bombs smother Baghdad. He considered me his equal or, at least, he pretended to. You read about child-actors who grow up around adults and, as a result, become drug addicts before puberty and unwittingly blurt out surprising truths. But then they're stupid, too, like they don't know simple things like which one is the gas pedal and which one is the brake pedal, and they've never had their own bank accounts, so you give them twenty bucks and they immediately go out and spend it all on rock candy and colored pencils. I was a little like that, only I *knew* I was like that, and I wanted to be different.

"I had to do it, Maxine," Hanson said. "That tree was Ricky's tree."

"Any tree could have been Ricky's tree."

"We planted that tree for Ricky."

"Well, it's gone, now." I resisted the urge to say, "Just like Ricky," and instead turned to look out the window and watch the night go by: a water tower, an oil derrick, a barbed-wire fence barely standing in a gulley full of mud. I remember thinking it was my fault Hanson decided to cut down Ricky's tree. Sometimes I still possess this same solipsistic need to demand attention when attention isn't due. Yesterday, after destroying my wristwatch, phone, and laptop computer, I had some regrets. The wristwatch had been a gift, the phone had come with a two-year contract, and, worst of all, I would have to go to work the next morning and explain away the laptop's demise with some lie about an accident or theft. I still haven't come up with a good excuse, so for now, I'm taking some time off work: strep throat, another lie.

* * *

That night, after Hanson cut down Ricky's the tree and we found ourselves at the locked gate of the city landfill, I fiddled with the radio knob until talk news came on, slumped down deep into the passenger seat of Hanson's truck, and said, "I hope you're happy."

"I am happy," he said. "Because now the bastards can't keep pretending they care."

In another story, Hanson's son Ricky might have been a reluctant marine killed by friendly fire during the first wave of Desert Storm. Or he might have been a boy my age, my first crush, the memory of his lips pressed to my neck still alive every time I walked past some old tree house in a vacant lot. Or he could have been a little boy, a cancer patient bravely wearing a Yankees cap to cover his fuzzy-bald head. But he wasn't any of those things. Ricky Hanson was forty-years-old, kind of a creep and definitely drowning in a fantasy of himself as an electric guitar player, still living at home and working as a custodian at the local high school. Two years prior, a vending machine in the teachers' lounge had fallen on him and crushed him to death. Hanson's wife, old and sick with grief, had died the following year.

That night, driving to the dump, I tried to cheer Hanson with one of those harmless platitudes you see on television movies featuring teenaged-boys lying dead in pearly-white coffins, their football jerseys newly ironed and their bodies barely cold.

"Everyone loved Ricky," I said. "The tree doesn't matter."

"They didn't love him," he said. "It's OK."

The high school principal had planted the tree in Ricky's honor. Only after the first frost had school officials invited Mr. and Mrs. Hanson to something called a Soil Sample Ceremony, a half-hour presentation and sob-fest after which members of the student body and the community at large were made to take away their own personal Ziploc bags containing frozen dirt from the base of Ricky's tree. Also, the principal's secretary ordered cling stickers for everyone's back windshield. Every now and then you still see one around town—Ricky Hanson: Pioneer Pride.

By then, my two older brothers and much older sister, already grown and out of the house, treated me as if I belonged in a catalog featuring Halloween masks and inflatable palm trees: fun to look at, but not exactly a top priority. My nearest brother—more like an uncle, really—played professional baseball. Everyone loved him. He brought me fancy soaps and hair barrettes on those rare occasions when he came home to visit. Sometimes I forgot what he looked like.

At the high school, I didn't have many friends. No one hated me, exactly—I was too boring to hate—but they thought me the kind of kid *good at dissection*—a fine lab partner, but bad for lunchroom chatter and shoplifting trips to the convenience store around the corner. On the blacktop, before and after school, I talked to a kid named Fadi Ammar— he and his parents were from Libya. Try moving to a small town in Oklahoma with a name like Fadi. Maybe his family pronounced it Faw-dee, but in the trumpet section of the Pioneer Pride Marching Band, it was Fatty. Even worse, he was actually a little bit fat. I felt sorry for him. I also had a friend named Bimbo, no lie. She was from Ghana and I felt sorry for her, too. I felt a little sorry for myself—people called me Maxi-pad and Maxwell Smart—but mostly I flew under the radar. Aside from Fadi and Bimbo and my array of elderly neighbors, I found company in books, and in the television news broadcasts I took way too seriously.

"You bring the tape?" Hanson said at his front door, about a week after he had cut down Ricky's tree. I had endured a rough day at school—the computer program, PETE, had given me a failing grade on my geometry exam, not called a geometry exam, but a "Sponge Activity." Did the consciousness lurking within PETE consider me a sponge and the geometry lesson a gallon of water I longed to absorb? In actual fact, I resembled a block of wood and the geometry lesson was like a lit match, or an electric drill, or a microwave oven. In any case, I had failed, and only sharp-eyed news analysis live from the Persian Gulf would cheer me up.

"Come in," Hanson said. "I have something to show you."

"You won't believe it," I said. "They're going after Israel."

"I heard," he said. "We'll turn up the volume while we're out in the yard."

"Why?"

"The trees," Hanson said. "I need to cut them all down."

I dropped the video tape on the coffee table and turned to face him. "You have to stop this," I said. "It's not going to help."

"Everything is clear, Maxine," he said. "For the first time, I see the future. I won't let them decide. The trees may be gone, but the tap roots, *the tap roots* will live on."

Since his wife died, Hanson had become increasingly reclusive, keeping the curtains closed during daylight hours, letting the newspapers pile up at the end of the driveway, and taking his pickup out of the garage only once a week—on Saturday mornings to buy groceries and visit the cigarette outlet store. One Saturday, he told me he had spent two hours browsing the long aisles of Walmart's hardware section, finally purchasing and bringing home several dozen plastic storage bins, fifty rolls of shelf paper, and a gas-powered chainsaw.

I followed him through the kitchen to the breakfast nook in the back corner of the house. The table, already set with a box of fiber cereal and a crystal vase with a single red rose, looked clean and neat, like a low-priced bistro. I knew Hanson was a little uptight—his cardigan sweaters, for example, always looked ironed, and, let's face it, nobody *irons* a cardigan sweater—but never before had I seen past the tidy confines of his living room. Later, he would tell me he owned a carpet rake, a plastic cleaning device the size of a golf club. With the carpet rake, Hanson knew the meaning of perfection. Like a widow brushing the stray hairs from her thousand and one cats, Hanson raked the carpet up and down, up and down. He positioned each piece of carpet in each individual rug so all fibers faced cardinal north, toward Canada and beyond. Before going to sleep every night, he raked the carpet in his bedroom all in the same direction: toward his final resting place. He raked and raked until he had raked himself into a corner. He removed his slippers and placed them under the bed. Then, he raked underneath where the slippers had been. Finally, when he was sure every inch of carpet had been raked in the exact same direction, he picked up the rake and tucked it underneath the blanket beside him, a talisman for comfort and desire. He told me all this only in his weakest moments, after three scotch and waters and an NBC interview with modernity's Alexander the Great. Stormin' Norman Schwarzkopf: we couldn't help but love him.

"I can't take it anymore, Maxine," he said. "I have to rid myself of all these extra—contraptions."

"Trees are not contraptions," I said. "They're trees."

"It's not just the trees," he said. All the extra blankets in the hall closet. When am I ever going to *use* them? And the board games, jeez. I haven't played *Risk* since 1975. I have to make some changes. I need some space to stretch out."

"You have a recliner," I said. "And a couch."

"It's a metaphor."

"And a hammock in the yard. Oh wait, you're cutting down the trees. I guess you don't have a hammock in the yard. Well, you *do* have a hammock in the yard, but you couldn't exactly *stretch out* in the thing, unless you wanted to lie on the ground and get all dirty."

You can see why people thought I was annoying. Hanson, preoccupied with the vision of his unencumbered future, hardly noticed. I followed him to the yard where he filled the thirsty chainsaw with gasoline.

"They're just in the way," he said. "Every time I mow the lawn, I have to duck to keep the branches from hitting me in the face."

"Just trim the branches, then."

"You don't get it, Maxine. I'm just not a tree *person* anymore. I used to be a tree person. I used to be the kind of person who planted this and that—oh my, look, this needs mulching, that needs watering, this needs a canopy to protect it from the sun. But I've realized they just get in the way. Everything gets in the way."

"In the way of what?"

"The lawn mower."

"I guess the *lawn* gets in the way of the lawn mower, too."

"Smart ass," he said. "You don't understand."

Next thing I knew he was using an Exact-o knife to cut down empty boxes from Sears so they were the exact right size for the garbage men to pick up the next morning.

"Anything over twelve inches and they leave you a nasty note," he said, piling branches and logs into a black hole that once held a refrigerator.

Inside, as Wolf Blitzer recounted the latest war dead, Hanson emptied all the contents of his hall closet into plastic storage bins with tight-fitting lids.

"You had dominoes?" I said.

"Sure," he said. "Cardinal Mexican Train. Why?"

"I thought you might teach me how to play."

"Too late," he said. On top of the dominoes he had placed *Scrabble, Clue,* and something called *Oh No, Not the Potato.* "This is all going to the Salvation Army."

"You know they make the poor people sign a prayer pledge to God before they give them anything? It's true."

"Guess I could take it to the elementary school."

"They're not allowed to play games," I said. "Unless they're on a computer."

"Here it is," he said. "My whole life. Most of it, anyway. Time to replace the shelf paper."

* * *

I never understood the importance of shelf paper. People say you need to keep a clean, smooth background upon which stray crumbs will make themselves visible. But who has *crumbs* in their hall closet? Yesterday, after smashing all my electronic equipment, I ate one of those high-energy protein bars and took a walk around the block. These days, I live with a woman nearly twenty years my senior. We have lived together for ten years now, and aside from our slightly skewed sense of mutual cultural history—she was six when Kennedy was shot and I've only heard the stories—we hardly notice the age difference. She does make more money than I do, so at Christmastime she buys me something like a leather arm chair and I buy her something like a book, but then, later, we share the chair and the book, and everything works out fine. In any case, we both hated Reagan, grew disaffected with Clinton, and shared the same strange, slow disbelief as we sat together watching television on that September morning in 2001. We still live in the same town where I grew up, though Hanson is long dead and the tree stumps in his yard have fallen to the ax.

And to be fair, I rely upon my girlfriend more than I should. True, I 'm happy to do things like open jars and kill spiders, but she has all the knowledge, all the experience. To this day, I don't know how to drive a car with a standard transmission. I cannot read maps. If products purchased from the local Walmart contain any kind of instructions, or warnings, or fine-printed caveats, I interrupt whatever she's doing and ask her to read every word of the little booklets printed in seven languages, leaving it entirely up to her to interpret the true meaning of phrases such as, "not for household use." And I'm afraid to make decisions. That's why everyone was so surprised when I smashed the wristwatch, phone, and laptop computer—all in the space of the same twelve hours.

Back in high school, my sense of duty prevented me from rash acts. One time—I was a sophomore, I think, and it was April Fool's Day—I made a phony announcement on the school's public address system—harmless, really, but I thought myself very brave. I had been assigned to read a flier about an upcoming band concert, Percy Granger's greatest hits. When the principal turned on the microphone, I read from the flier just as I was supposed to, but then continued by saying the principal's secretary had given me the late-breaking announcement that school would be dismissed ten minutes early. Since school was to be let out in a mere fifteen minutes anyway, the principal allowed my prank to pass without punishment and my classmates considered me heroic.

That same day, in the ten minutes I otherwise would have been sitting inside listening to PETE give a lecture about the quadratic formula, I instead stood outside on the black-top talking to Fadi and Bimbo about the trumpet section's upcoming playoffs. Fadi said he was destined to get last chair and Bimbo said she was switching to the flute, anyway, and I said I'd never learn to hit that stupid high C, and Hanson, walking a dog I had never seen before, approached the empty patch of ground where Ricky's tree had once stood. Since the war ended, I had stopped going over to his house in the evenings. And I had grown up some, too—already I had my learner's permit and soon I would have my driver's license—so spending a lot of time with my octogenarian neighbor started to seem embarrassing. If he was my grandfather or something, sure, but he was just my neighbor, and quickly ours turned into the kind of relationship where you wave while standing at the mailboxes and give each other the thumbs up when the clouds looked like rain. That day at the high school, while he stood there before Ricky's tree stump with the dog I'd never seen, his legs wobbled, his hands shook, and his narrow shoulders seemed to disappear inside the great tent of his neatly-pressed cardigan sweater. I thought of him at home, tucked into bed with his carpet rake, dreaming. I told Fadi and Bimbo I would catch up with them later.

"What's the dog's name?" I said.

"Maxine," he said. "No, I mean, hi, Maxine. Bing. The dog's name is Bing. Like Bing Crosby. It's stupid, I know."

"It's not that stupid."

The dog, a French bulldog wearing one of those doggy outfits—a suit collar with a necktie attached—wriggled and ran, testing the end of Hanson's leash. Hanson called to the dog in a tense, mock whisper, but Bing caught wind of a candy bar wrapper a few feet away and refused to listen. "School's out early," he said. "Is it a holiday or something?"

"Sort of," I said. "Don't worry, though, I won't tell anyone you're here."

"The dog needed a walk," he said. "We're on our way to the park."

"He's handsome," I said. "How long you had him?"

"A while," he said. "Hey, I'm getting rid of some old news magazines. You want 'em?"

"Sure," I said. "I'll come over some time."

"I'll have them for you," he said. He reeled in the leash and turned to leave. "Well, bye, I guess."

"Hey, Hanson," I said. He was almost gone. "You get rid of all of Ricky's stuff?"

He turned. In the sunlight, I could make out the corners of his mouth turning soft—upward or downward I couldn't tell—but the sound of his voice changed from hollow and sharp to easy and low. "Everything's gone," he said. "Everything but his electric guitar. I hate that goddamned thing."

For a minute, I thought of what it must have been like, while Ricky was alive, Hanson reading a news magazine and eating his fiber cereal, Ricky, upstairs and angry, practicing "The Star-Spangled Banner" over and over again, Mrs. Hanson, beleaguered as always, scrubbing bacon grease from a frying pan. And probably Hanson yelled and Mrs. Hanson cried and Ricky kept on wailing away.

"I'll come over," I said. "For the news magazines."

"Good," he said. "I'll have them in chronological order."

Even though Hanson was more than fifty years my senior, I thought I understood everything about him. I knew he missed Ricky. I knew he missed his wife. I knew he liked current events and once liked board games and gardening. So what makes a person cut down trees and get rid of all his old belongings? Madness, I thought. An aberration.

* * *

I'll tell you what happened, and I'll start with the wristwatch. Well, I'll start with my current neighbors. For a while, I thought they would be like the Hansons, old and weird, but kind. They are old and weird, and at first they seemed very kind—they brought over a plate of brownies on the day we moved in—but then we saw their picture in the paper for The Society for the Sanctity of Marriage picnic. So now I always think they're looking at me, and even though they probably were out running errands the day I had the problem with the wristwatch, I imagined they were staring out their front window, making gagging sounds as I jogged by. The battery died. The battery died and I became angry. Rather than removing the watch and putting it in my pocket for safe keeping, or, even more sensibly, just jogging along without looking at the watch, I yanked at the strap and threw the whole thing down in the street.

And I'll tell you what day it was. My partner, girlfriend, whatever, and my father share the same birthday, and it was their birthday, when all this happened. My father was turning eighty and my partner, girlfriend, whatever, was turning fifty. Neither is the type to make a fuss, so the four of us were just planning to go out to dinner some other night that week. But I started thinking about how my father used to ride the bus to get medicine for his younger sister and about how my partner, girlfriend, my dear, can walk out into a field of horses and make them follow her to the gate. And I started to miss them before they were gone.

And about the cell phone: my girlfriend was having some problems at work. These problems, they kept her up at night and worried her terribly, literally, I'm sure, taking years from her life. So when she called from work to say she would be home late, and the battery died before I could tell her happy birthday, I crushed the phone underneath the weight of a forty-pound dumbbell. And later, when I emailed my father to say something like *I haven't enjoyed my own birthday for a while now* and he replied to say something like, *You have a lot more birthdays to go than I do, so you had better buck up,* again I became angry, not at my father, but at the computer for locking up every time I tried to save his email message in a folder marked "Dad." And that's when I went to the garage for a baseball bat and hit the computer square in the middle of the screen, three strikes, out. And even though I think Hanson was stupid to cut down Ricky's tree, I can see why he did it, too. I recently read about a climatologist who spent every April Fool's Day planting trees with his grandchildren. Hanson didn't have any grandchildren, of course, and if you listen to the climatologists, there's really nothing left to do but cut down a tree here and there, to let the world know you stand for something, to make money along with the money-makers, to throw up your hands and proclaim goddamnit all to hell I guess the ship's going down.

Lab Report

Since the advent of the twenty-first century and since the onset of the great recession in particular, employers have seen a marked increase in non-lethal, work-related stress injuries along with billable conditions such as carpal tunnel syndrome, rheumatoid arthritis, chronic fatigue, migraine, and glaucoma. Employers in the new economy face an uncertain workplace landscape fraught with potential pitfalls: these injuries and chronic conditions, in addition to the obvious drawbacks of increased absenteeism, slowed productivity, and heightened liability risk, also represent a larger cultural shift away from the core, bedrock principles of hard work and self-reliance and toward a dependence on the softer, and ultimately more sinister, tentacles of the great and powerful octopus knows as the nanny state.

During the months and years immediately following 9/11, faculty and staff in the Bartlett Center and Morrill and Thatcher Halls on the campus of Oklahoma State University in Stillwater reported in a voluntary survey to Blue Cross Blue Shield of Oklahoma a 13% increase in shortness of breath, a 28% increase in dental cavities, and, perhaps most troubling of all since there is no known cure, a 34% increase in cases of eczema extreme enough to force the patient to wear only long sleeves. Researchers on the Oklahoma State University campus, working in conjunction with Blue Cross Blue Shield, hypothesized an increase in positive energy surrounding each patient along with consistent, sterile application of a prescription hydrocortisone cream would reduce eczema rates among the faculty and staff. In a double-blind study, researchers posing as nurse practitioners at the Bud Seretean Center for Wellness advised patients first on the practice of documented *medical* self-care, and second on the practice of documented *spiritual* self-care. Researchers established three control groups: the first was comprised of patients receiving only instructions on correct application of the hydrocortisone cream, the second was comprised of patients receiving only a pamphlet about the various Sunday church services available in the Payne County area, and the third and final control group, smaller and less-afflicted by comparison, consisted of patients who were told they were there to watch a short video about bicycle safety.

"This is a bunch of shit," one of the patients—male patient #62—said. "I haven't ridden a bicycle since I was six years old."

Another male patient agreed: "Yeah, next thing ya know we'll have to listen to that lady lawyer lecture us about sexual harassment again."

These patients, along with those silently watching the

safety video, all were made to sign a document including the words "hold harmless" and "university or representative of the university" and an explicit directive that bicycle helmets were mandatory within ten feet of a crosswalk, and further admonishments as to how crosswalks were there for pedestrians anyway, and the final declaration that those deciding not to wear bicycle helmets were doing so at their own risk. These signed documents were passed along to the office of risk management, after which they were kept on file for the duration of the patients' employment at Oklahoma State University, Board of Regents for the Oklahoma Agricultural and Mechanical Colleges, 220 Student Union, Legal Counsel, there to protect you, not to suspect you.

The results of the study were mixed. On the one hand, patients receiving both the medical and spiritual guidance showed a 4% decrease in symptoms (with an error rate of plus or minus 1%) as compared to those in the bicycle safety control group, but the patients receiving only the Sunday services pamphlet *also* showed a decrease in symptoms at the exact same rate. Those receiving only the hydrocortisone cream fared best of all, as several patients in this group reported at least two days of the five-day workweek as "mostly symptom-free" and several more reported feeling well enough to return to their previous practice of taking advantage of casual Fridays by wearing short sleeves.

The overall decrease in symptoms among all patients in the study indicated a possible placebo effect, but patients reporting a decrease in symptoms were asked to fill out a survey indicating the source of their improved condition. Of those survey respondents, only 8% attributed their wellness to the hydrocortisone cream, while a striking 82% attributed their wellness to "unknown factors" or "factors beyond their control." Increased spiritual awareness, in this case, may not have cured Oklahoma State University of the scourge of eczema, but, as this study documents, prayer, prayer-guidance, and other surrogates showed a direct relationship with increased states of wellness, overall skin-softening, and an increase in productivity due to fewer doctor visits and less time spent engaging in workplace itching. To counteract the so-called "clever Hans" effect in which subjects perform certain tasks only because they're receiving subtle or unconscious cues from their testers, patients wore blindfolds when they responded to previously recorded audio of prayer-related survey questions. At the conclusion of the audio survey, patients were allowed to remove their blindfolds and take turns going to the restroom. Those who remained in the testing room until the conclusion of the session each were asked to write a short paragraph about the emotional effects of prayer and prayer-surrogacy. One patient's paragraph stood out to researchers not just for its intensity but also for its overwhelming sense of gratitude; for scientists, even those their contemporaries might call "mad," work always with the goal of advancing the progress of mankind. With that in mind, the authors of this study will conclude this report with the unedited text of Patient #62's paragraph on the emotional effects of prayer and prayer-guidance; after you read it, I'm sure you will agree with the authors of this study when they say his paragraph is itself a kind of prayer, and further, I'm sure you will answer the call for us all to join together with equal measures humility and might so that we may defeat the powers of big government and make sure his prayer does not go unanswered.

The Emotional Effects of Prayer and Prayer-Guidance, by Patient #62:

I haven't ridden a bicycle since I was six years old. But I tell you, I'd like to start riding again. I can't remember the last time I spent all afternoon outdoors, unless you count the time I mowed my lawn last week, something you hardly need to do anymore since it never rains and the grass never grows. Texas is on fire. A thousand houses: whoosh, gone. I work so many long hours I feel like a factory worker in charge of the assembly line producing a living warehouse for factory workers for the next generation of factories, and they, too, will produce factory workers, if they're lucky, or maybe they'll just rot. The other day I thought of that commonplace urging busy people to stop and smell the roses, and then I remembered my roses are dead. So I haven't really thought about the emotional effects of prayer and prayer-guidance, but I'd like to ride a bike again someday, and maybe if my arms weren't so itchy, maybe if I could get out of here before 7:00 every night, maybe if I didn't have to spend so much time in the company of my stuffed-shirted colleagues and their bad tastes in foreign food and foreign films, maybe, just maybe, I would ride my bike off into the proverbial sunset, hotter than it used to be, sure, but at least I'd be able to say "eat my dust" and mean it, my hands gripping the handlebars, my eyes facing the wind, the whole world in front of me and Oklahoma nothing but a distant memory, a pile of brush on the curbside, a trickle of water where a creek used to be.

Envelope

Most days he felt ill. In the morning, he woke feeling sick to his stomach, and every evening, by the time the day's events and three bland meals had softened the sharp edges of his digestive tract, his head began to ache, at first a dull, ruthless pressure between his eyes, then a blind spot in the middle of his vision, and finally, an all-encompassing shift in his center of gravity. The only cure was a drink and two Tylenol, followed by television, and more sleep.

And he was cold. Every morning he was cold, and every evening, he shivered in rigid misery underneath a fake fur blanket on the sofa in the living room. But in the afternoon, for just one minute every day, he was warm—not too warm, but just warm enough to roll up his sleeves and open a window on the other side of the house. One day in winter, just after the mail was delivered at 3:15, he stood at the window overlooking his back yard. In the stack of mail he found nothing interesting: phone bill, garbage bill, a couple of credit card offers. His elderly father had given him a surprise subscription to *Time* magazine. But out the window, in the shade between the house and the hammock, he saw something unusual, extraordinary even, something that might make him feel better, forever.

It was a red envelope. A red envelope! What could be inside? He knew one fifth of the world's population celebrated Chinese New Year, a chance to buy new clothes, eat good food, and exchange red envelopes with cash tucked beneath the center flap. He consulted a calendar, a freebie from his insurance company, affixed to the side of the refrigerator with a magnet. Tomorrow—hooray for tomorrow—was the first day of the Chinese New Year, the Year of the Pig. Once, while still employed at the Center for Global Investment and Developing Technology, he placed an order for ballpoint pens with a company in California. Because of the Chinese New Year, the pens arrived late, too late for him to try one out before quitting his job the following month. But now he might benefit from the Chinese New Year, he might collect. He donned a jacket and started for the back door.

Outside, acorns littered the patio. To find himself in such sweet light, to discover the day's events shifting somehow to accommodate an unfulfilled wish, to feel the warm air against his skin and to watch as the wind blew an empty milk carton across the fence line—all of these filled him with hope and possibility. All he really wanted in life was for someone to say, *I'm sorry that happened to you* or *You deserve better*. No one ever said those things, though, so he had to content himself with superficial standing among the world's grabbers and pleasers: I would like to win an unexpected prize—ten thousand dollars and a bouquet of balloons. I would like a car in the garage that not only runs reliably but also tells onlookers tales of success and prosperity. I would like a wife who willingly attends sporting events and children without holes in their bodies. I would like to fit in.

He had none of these things, of course. Instead, he had an old, dead dog buried somewhere in the back yard. He had a brother in New Mexico and a sister in South Dakota and a father right here in town, in an apartment complex meant for people too wealthy for nursing homes, too proud to move in with their adult children, and too helpless to live on their own. His mother was dead and he himself had never married. For many years he went on dates—to dance clubs and restaurants and foreign films. Then, one day, when the woman across from him at dinner began to weep, he decided to give up. She was crying, really crying. She was so lonely, she said. Even in the presence of others, especially in the presence of others, she felt so alone. He offered her a handkerchief and promised to take her home, right away, so that her embarrassment would fade. Don't you understand, she said. There's nowhere to go.

Now in his back yard, the red envelope signaled a shake-up. He realized he expected a similar change in the status quo every day when the mail came: today might be the day. Of course he received only consumer confidence surveys and coupons for items he never would buy. But still, every day, he hoped.

In the yard next door, he saw a tree house, newly-built since the last time he had bothered to look. Had he failed to overhear the buzz of saws and the swing of hammers, the aerodynamic rush of lumber scraps and tree branches as they fell to the ground? He looked closer. This was not a tree house, but a house without a tree, a clapboard cubicle wedged on top of three tall stilts, like a beach house built too close to the shore. Everything was like that. A tree house was not a tree house. The Chinese New Year was not the Chinese New Year. The red envelope was not a red envelope, but a flier advertising new, low rates for satellite TV. Lately he had been having trouble with his cable television—the picture skipped and certain channels, instead of playing the regularly scheduled sound, rang with a deafening, pulsing beep. Maybe he needed to replace the cable with a brand new, shiny satellite poised on the edge of his roof. Finally, a change: this is what he was after, this is what he found. Inside, after dialing the phone number on the flier, he held the receiver away from his ear, the butterfly ring-ring-ring echoing throughout the kitchen, every inch of the world awash in the golden hum of expectation.

Photo Album

One of the customers ran over Susanna's dog. Only recently had she become what they called a dog person, though she was ill, recovering from a stay in the hospital for broken bones and a secondary infection, forced to hire a friend's teenaged daughter to walk the dog and bring in the mail. Growing up, though, she had never been a dog person. Neither was she what they called a "people person." She enjoyed the dubious distinction of rising every day before the sun came up, a morning person, though she kept it a secret so as not to appear puritanical or dull.

She was up in time for the early show the morning after her dog died in the street. Anger rose in her chest when she thought of the lemonade-drinker puckering his lips as he stomped on the brakes late, too late to notice her Australian Shepherd dashing after a squirrel, his leash trailing off like a kite's tail behind him. She didn't know which customer had been responsible—could have been anyone, really, the line was so long—and her injury kept her from undertaking the fruitless pursuit of criminal investigation. The whole set-up was strange, too, since most normal people didn't like to drink lemonade in December. It was one of those rules: fresh vegetables in July, hot chocolate in January, red wine in winter, and lemonade stands run by greedy, pint-sized capitalists, their hand-painted signs advertising watered-down refreshment in June, July, and August, a rip-off and a smile all summer long.

To run a lemonade stand in December seemed to her not only ill advised but also stupid and inconsiderate, like those parents who tried to sell their sons' Cub Scout popcorn at work. And now that one of the lemonade-drinkers had killed her dog, she nursed a grudge against the neighbors, the neighbors' children, all the customers, and lemonade itself, a poison, like antifreeze or gasoline.

Her dog-walker was named Lynette. Lynette was sixteen and serious, the daughter of a co-worker, an honors student, the star goalie on the citywide soccer team and an intern in the office of a Democratic state senator. She had seemed trustworthy enough. The morning after the dog's death, Susanna sent the girl a text message to deliver the bad news, her walking papers so to speak, her services no longer required, thanks, she said, for all your help. Had the girl sense enough to hold tight to the leash or even run in the opposite direction, the dog would have obeyed and kept his life. Susanna had told her this much right after it happened. She had been watching a tasteless "Holidazzle" Christmas parade on television, and, hearing the screech and scream just ten feet from her bedroom window, she scrambled for the door and hobbled outside on her crutches to see her dog's motionless body in the street. The car drove away. No one thought to check for the license plate number, and Lynette, crying and gulping with great, voluminous waves of panic, drew more attention from sympathetic onlookers than did either Susanna or her dead dog. But the dog did not suffer, and he was old, in any case, almost too old to be chasing after squirrels in the first place, and when the car slammed against his chest, his breath was taken from him in an instant, like an exploding light bulb on the cobwebbed ceiling of some old garage.

Still, Susanna missed him, and it was not lost on her that while she herself had been hit by a car and lived, the dog had been hit by a car and died. Three months before, she'd been on a bicycle, riding illegally and in the wrong direction on the shoulder of a state highway, when the twentysomething farm kid driving bales of hay to his grandpa's cattle ranch reached for his sunglasses in the cup-holder of his truck before grazing her rear tire. It was the fall into the ravine that broke her collarbone and fractured her femur—and she ultimately concluded he'd been lying about the sunglasses and was in fact reaching for his phone—but she had lived to tell the tale, and she felt guilty, somehow, because her poor old dog, out for a jaunt in his very own neighborhood, had not.

Now, it turned out, the driver of the truck—the boy who not three months ago had sent her to the hospital and, strangely, visited her every day clutching a single, helium balloon—was also her dog-walker's new boyfriend, an unsurprising coincidence in this backwater town. Stuff like that was always happening: the mayor who also drove the school bus, the accountant who moonlighted at Walmart, the police officer neighbor who should have given you a break but didn't when he pulled you over for speeding. Worse, the dog-walker's mother, Susanna's only close friend from the public library where they both worked, offered to pay Susanna three hundred bucks plus a sizeable Walmart gift card to photograph the happy couple for the dog-walker's senior prom. Though the girl's name was Lynette, Susanna, both in the privacy of her own thoughts and in public to the girl's own mother, called her The Dog-Walker and her boyfriend Balloon Boy, named after a flash-in-the-pan media sensation, the seven or eight-year-old boy whose father had lied about his disappearance in the basket of a weather balloon with the hope of scoring the family's own reality television show. The nickname, a dual nod to the young man's odd, daily presence at the hospital and the duplicitous nature of his original scam, did not seem to bother Susanna's coworker, since she admitted to thinking her daughter could do better. And now that Susanna was out of the hospital, he visited her at the library on Tuesday and Thursday afternoons, still clutching his single, strange helium balloon, which he never offered to Susanna but called on her to admire nonetheless. Judging from the hair falling into his eyes and the cowboy hat he always wore, even indoors, Balloon Boy probably didn't even own a pair of sunglasses, much less keep them in the cup holder of his stupid farm truck. But a cell phone? These days you rarely met someone without one.

Now Susanna's leg had improved to the point she no longer needed crutches, and she wondered if hiding behind the camera, poised and ready on a tripod, might keep Balloon Boy from feeling the need for his customary prop. But her

history with The Dog Walker would only add to the ten-
sion, so that the room would fairly well buzz with resentment and dread. But Lynnette would pretend to be happy
to see her, offering an insincere hug, making false attempts
at flattery with sweet-sounding observations about Susanna's outfit or hair. Lynnette's mother had arranged to conduct the photo shoot in the alcove of the public library, an
odd, but neutral choice, since the photographs were bound
to feature either a bust of some dead white man or a map
of the world somewhere off in the background. But Susanna felt confident she could make the happy couple appear
glamorous, on the precipice of some unnamable success,
like young stars making the leap from their roles on the
Disney Channel to mainstream movies and leading spots
on the talk show circuit.

For Susanna, photography had started off as a hobby, but
she was good enough to score a summer full of weddings and
the occasional commercial gig shooting stuff like the Parade
of Homes and bowls of cottage cheese.

"You look beautiful," she said to Lynnette, and she meant
it. She refused to meet the gaze of Balloon Boy. "That dress
is a stunner."

"Thanks," she said. "I got in on Ebay."

"*I* got it on Ebay," Balloon Boy said. "Connections."

Lynnete's mother made small talk about the cost of the
dress, the cost of the shoes, the cost of the steak dinner before
the prom. Susanna was used to people bragging about their
expenditures, but she surprised herself by joining in. Together,
they spoke of the cost of chicken versus steak, the cost of the
corsage, the cost of hair and make-up, the cost of the prom's

rental space, the cost of hiring teachers to chaperone, free, it turned out, since they were made to volunteer. Twenty minutes had passed, and Susanna hadn't taken a single picture.

"You're slowing them down," Lynette's mother said. "Who would have dreamt a photo shoot could take so long."

"You want to get your money's worth," Susanna said. "I don't come cheap."

"Don't I know it."

"Mom," Lynette said. "Could you please leave?"

"Shut up now," her mother said. "I've spent eighteen years and nine months waiting for this moment." Today, it turned out, was Lynette's birthday.

"Great," Susanna said, taking the first photo. "Now you can vote."

"She'd better not vote," Balloon Boy said. "Not for Obama. Not for Hillary, either."

"Obama already won," Susanna said. "Twice. And Hillary already lost. Twice."

"I know," he said. "But in case one of them comes out of retirement and runs for dictator or head of the one-world government or something."

"Smile," Susanna said. "Say cheese."

"Fontina," Lynette said.

"Velveeta," Balloon Boy said.

"I taught them that joke," Lynette's mother said. "They love me."

Things went on for a while in the usual fashion—Susanna asked them to sit, stand up again, stare at the ceiling as if it were heaven above. She took a long series in which Balloon Boy pretended to tie the corsage's ribbon around Lynette's slim white wrist. The truth was the whole thing was boring, like watching a PowerPoint presentation or entering the end stages of a game of Scrabble you knew you were going to lose. She was more or less confident she had enough shots to put together a pretty good package, perfect for photo album, when she had an idea.

"Oh no," she said. "My memory card."

Lynette and her mother both froze in terror, but Balloon Boy, who seemed to understand this as a sign to take a much-needed break, departed for the vending machine in the library's break room. Lynette's voice rose in panic, and her mother grabbed the camera from Susanna's hand.

"Everything's gone," Susanna lied. "They'll have to come back tomorrow."

"Tomorrow?" Lynette's mother said. "But the prom is tonight."

"They'll have to come by after their little—parties—then," Susanna said. "I'd planned to stay here all night to do some re-shelving anyway."

"This is crazy," Lynette said. "We can't take our prom photos *after* the prom."

"In the morning," Susanna said. "I work best in the morning."

By this time, Balloon Boy had returned with a Mountain Dew and a bag of Cheetos, his fingers coated with a fine, orange dust. "What's going on?" he said.

Lynette began to cry. For a moment, Susanna saw herself in the girl's despair, and she remembered, in a flash, the desperate and sudden pitfalls of the required rituals of young adulthood. Only no one had asked *her* to go to a prom, not once. Always on prom night she'd rented a movie or taken a walk around town alone. Later, in college, her first serious boyfriend would take a dubious pleasure in her dateless high school years, as if he'd been the first to climb not a mountain but a rocky hill littered with bottle caps in some boyhood friend's backyard. Now she wanted revenge, not on her first serious boyfriend, not on all those high school boys who'd failed to notice her, not even on Balloon Boy's negligence that day on the highway or Lynette's stupidity in allowing her poor old dog to get killed. She wanted revenge on youth itself, its heedless stretch across the cultural landscape, its hunger, its all-pervasive need. That she herself wasn't getting any younger might seem like a sign of mere envy, but it was more than that; she was angry, and she knew she deserved some lasting attention, or at least a nod in her direction. No one noticed her in youth, and no one noticed her still.

After a series of negotiations in which Susanna would not budge, Balloon Boy and Lynette finally went off to the prom, and Lynette's mother went home. They all agreed the happy couple would reappear at the library's back door at exactly 5:30 the next morning. During the prom itself, Susanna went shopping. It took her eight trips to and from the grocery store, eight trips in which her backseat was completely full and the view from her rearview mirror was impossibly blocked, but by the time she was finished, the library's alcove was packed with the electrified energy of exactly 55 helium balloons, all of them red with red ribbons attached. She made a final trip to the store and back for straight pins, a plastic pitcher, a wooden spoon, a small bag of sugar, and, of course, a packet of lemonade.

"Let us in," Lynette said from the alleyway. They were early by an hour or more, but Susanna was prepared, and having Lynette's mother out of the way would liberate the process from the prying eyes of adulthood. "Our pictures," Lynette said. Her pounding knock was like a cop's. "We're ready to make memories."

"Speak for yourself," Balloon Boy said after Susanna had unlocked and propped open the door "I feel like shit." His face was puffy and his eyes were bloodshot, both obvious products of the evening's revelry, rented hotel rooms, maybe, a punchbowl spiked with something stronger. Lynette appeared more or less preserved, like a doll enclosed in glass. She was the driver, she told Susanna; always she obeyed the rules of traffic.

"Of course you do," Susanna said. "So responsible."

Balloon Boy's rumpled clothing reeked of cigarette smoke, though Lynette seemed neither to notice nor care. She doted on him as much as or more than she had before the prom, and her cooing attentions hardened Susanna's resolve. Bypassing the alcove, she directed them to the reference section, a row of tasteful dictionary stands in the background. For a while, she pretended—the memory card *and* the batteries removed from her camera—to take the standard set of romantic tributes, the usual poses of the young and in love. She directed Balloon Boy to hold Lynette, kiss Lynette, kneel in front of Lynette, gaze into her eyes. So far, the helium balloons in the alcove remained hidden from view.

"The alcove," she said finally. "I need you two lovebirds to see what I have set up for you in the alcove."

They followed her into the crowded hallway; the balloons took up so much space it was difficult for the three of them to stand for very long without ducking or shifting. The whole thing was very funny, and before long they all began to laugh.

"Pop them," Susanna said, handing each one a straight pin. "Pop the balloons."

Lynnette spoke first, "But why?" she said. "I'm sorry, Susanna, but this is weird."

"Pop the goddamned balloons," she said. "This is part of the photo shoot."

"I'm not going to pop them," Balloon Boy said. "You pop them."

"Look," Susanna said, grabbing her own straight pin and taking the first stabbing shot. "It's easy."

POP, went the balloon, and all three were stunned into silence.

"Now," Susanna said. "Your turn."

They were reluctant at first, their hands shaking in rhythm with Lynette's nervous laughter. But they complied with her wishes: *pop, pop, pop,* the pinprick attacks no longer hesitant, more confident now, becoming frenzied and rushed. After the last burst of energy, all the balloons were finished off, dead soldiers on the alcove floor, like the final day of the circus or a clown's precursor to suicide. Susanna, though she would never be beautiful, never again be young, had this one moment of triumph, the satisfaction that came from the gunshot-sound of each balloon's last, lifeless spark, the pleasure of taking the only actual picture she would take all night, the comic photo of the boy's stone-faced silence and the girl's perplexed awe, the two of them standing among the red rubber ruins in the alcove. And with her vision of the photograph came the knowledge she'd made something happen, for once, and she grew calm with the true fact of her power. Now she took up the pitcher and two Styrofoam cups. If only she'd thought to buy bendable straws.

"Pucker up, you two," she said. "You must be thirsty."

Dress Rehearsal

Joan always said I was a cretin—and maybe she was right—but it wasn't my fault no one ever took me to a museum. My parents' tastes in home décor included my father's collection of duck decoys and my mother's collection of porcelain dolls, and the only book on the lone, slim shelf in the living room was the *Good News Bible*. Again: not my fault. They didn't go to plays. They didn't take photographs. They didn't have a garden. All day long, my father perched on a short stool in the ladies' shoe department at JC Penney, his fingers sore from trying to wedge last year's penny loafers onto the swollen feet of our principal's secretary, a woman of modest means who somehow still managed a very reliable weekly shopping trip to Cimarron Plaza. Every night, my father went home to the sight of my mother, exhausted from her long day spent mucking out stalls and stacking square bales, listening to Waylon Jennings wide-ass open and cooking corned beef hash from a can. Sometimes two cans. Sometimes we went out, but not often.

Joan said I was a diamond-in-the-rough, but she had a large heart and a soft spot for the locals. This is Oklahoma we're talking about, and not a university town, not exactly, certainly not Tulsa or Oklahoma City, but the humble Rogers county outpost called Claremore. Probably you've seen—or at least heard the soundtrack to—*Oklahoma!*. Generally those old tunes provided more than enough information for out-of-towners. We did not host box socials, nor did we spontaneously burst into song, but we did care about bullshit-stuff like the wicked ways of interlopers, whether or not the farmer and the cowman should be friends, and, believe it or not, the presence or absence of Mr. Bluebird on our shoulders. Art imitated life, Joan always said, and life, in this case, was a faded Technicolor movie without much dialogue.

Joan was the high school librarian, and I, she claimed, was her most voracious reader. She called me a cretin only for comic effect, and also because she called all the honors students cretins and because I failed to qualify as a National Merit Scholar. Those tests were not made for Oklahomans. And I called her Joan not because we were big buddies but because her last name was Gawky, and—probably because she really *was* gawky—she asked everyone from the principal to the third floor janitor to call her Joan. The word on the street was that sometime before 1988 everyone called her *Miss* Joan, but something about Reagan's reelection made her decide to drop the old-fashioned formality.

So when my parents took my sister and me to the early showing of *Predator 2* at the Satellite Twin in Cowboy Mall, I did not expect to see Joan there with her friends from the university. You could tell they were from the university because the men had beards, the unsmiling women carried quilted purses, and the kids, two of them teenagers and a third much younger, wore extra-dark blue jeans, last year's basketball shoes, and matching T-shirts that said, "Eat Whole Grains." Joan flagged me down in the ticket line and introduced me as "Charlotte of Mecklenburg-Strelitz," to which all the kids replied, "cool."

"It's really Bair," I said."Charlotte Bair. You all come to see *Predator 2?*"

"Oh *god* no," Joan said."We're here for frozen yogurt before the protest."

I should amend what I said earlier about Claremore. It's in the middle of what they call "Green Country,"—not because it's all that green; rather because it's not quite as burnt-out brown as the rest of the state—and does in fact claim the dubious distinction of its own university, known as Rogers State in the official sense, and, for those of us with more imagination, Hillcat High. That year—it was 1990, two years after the movie came out in theaters—a group of students on campus wanted to host a screening of the controversial *The Last Temptation of Christ*. The administration refused, and everyone with a brain knew it was censorship. The rallying cry, "Show the Movie!" took on its own rebellious, self-important cachet; if you believed in artistic freedom, as a select group of us high school juniors did, you wanted to see the brutality of the crucifixion not just once or twice but as many times as possible, and the more the church people recoiled in horror the better. That night, the night of the official opening of *Predator 2*, unbeknownst to my poor parents and me, there also was a Show the Movie! March on the Hillcat High campus, and more than anything I wanted to ditch my family to join Joan and the Whole Grain Gang for an event I was sure would look and feel exactly like Woodstock, only with better food and more bales of hay.

"Joan," I said, suddenly embarrassed I'd been caught wanting to see such pedestrian fare as *Predator 2*. "Do you think they're going to show the movie after all?"

"They're afraid," she said. "But they shouldn't be."

By then my parents were well ahead of me in the line for popcorn, and, as far as I could tell, they had not yet noticed my absence. I considered telling a lie, that my parents really were there to see *Rosencrantz & Guildenstern Are Dead* and I was there only to drop them off and pick them up after the movie was over, but I knew Joan would see through such a charade, and so decided to tell the truth.

"My dad's a big Gary Busey fan," I said. "It's his birthday." I pointed to my sister at the candy counter; the attendant was loading her up with Milk Duds and a soda the size of a trashcan. "My sister," I said. "You remember her."

Joan looked past me to the line forming outside the ladies' room. "I don't believe I've seen your sister at the library of late."

We're fraternal twins, but nothing alike: in those years, I dreamt of going into politics or law, and my pious twin, who'd already decided she was getting married instead of going to college, spent most of her time sorting used clothing at the thrift store sponsored by our church. I shrugged and turned to Joan. "We might go to the arcade after."

"Isn't that lovely," Joan said. "A celebration."

"It's OK," I said. "My dad's a diabetic, though." Immediately I knew I'd been an idiot for blurting out yet another embarrassment, an unnecessary piece of medical history that kept us all from ever enjoying anything but the most bland, sugar-free desserts at home. In the mini-van on the way to the movie, my sister had talked non-stop about this, her one chance to drink real Coke in the theater's air-conditioned splendor, and I knew she'd be salivating over the frozen yogurt stand when we passed it on the way back to the parking lot after the movie. But perhaps Joan would feel sorry for me and my diabetic father and invite me to another protest on another night, something on a larger scale, something with tear gas and pigs.

Just then, one of the Whole Grain Children, a red-headed boy who looked about ten or twelve, said, "This will be my first frozen yogurt. Ever."

Obviously, he failed to appreciate the importance of expressing his rights to free speech. "This is Samuel," Joan said. "He's having quite the celebration himself."

The bearded men and the unsmiling women shuffled along toward the door, and though all three kids lingered behind them, Joan did not appear to mind them, and, in fact, appeared hostile to the older boy, also a red-head, and though I did not recognize him from school, I assumed he was a sophomore at least, since he had his own wallet on a chain that hung from the pocket of his oversized jeans. Looking more closely at his T-shirt, I saw that he'd added a parenthetical notation in black Magic Marker, so that it read, "Eat Whole Grains (And After That, Eat Shit and Die)." Immediately, I wanted him to become my boyfriend. But Joan and The Whole Grain Gang departed before I found out his name. The third child, a girl, was not a red head but a blonde, younger than me I was sure, but possibly a couple of years older than the one called Samuel. That night she appeared sickly, thinner than the others, and more remote. She clung to one of the unsmiling women and asked for a cough drop from her purse. I would learn later that Joan was their great aunt, though all three children, even the two gingers, were cousins to one another and not siblings. I imagined myself their fun-loving neighbor, the one who brought exciting snacks to their pool parties, a reliable source of diversion and the originator of all their favorite inside jokes.

"I don't really like movies," I said. "I'd rather read the book."

"Sequels," the girl said. "The worst."

That summer, I saw Joan and the Whole Grain Gang around town two or three more times, but never would I be allowed to attend a Show The Movie! Protest, and never, in fact, did they actually show the movie on the Rogers State campus. In the fall, on a night when my parents were scheduled to attend my sister's piano recital, I faked a sore throat and walked to the video store instead. I made popcorn and everything, a private showing, but ended up falling asleep well before the crucifixion. By the time I came to, my parents and sister were due home at any moment, so I had no choice but to eject the tape before it was over—I was not kind; I did not rewind—and sneak it back to the video store the next day.

That year in the cafeteria—my sister and I now were seniors who "ruled the school"—Joan had been reduced to lunchroom monitor and all-purpose disciplinarian. The library had faced unprecedented budget cuts, and there was a shortage of new books to catalog, though the technology budget was more robust than ever. I was used to seeing Joan in the library, but her new station in the cafeteria unnerved me, especially after I realized her primary responsibility was to hover over the trashcans and discourage students from throwing away their uneaten fruits and vegetables. It seemed beneath her somehow, and I was ashamed to go near her.

"Well, if it isn't the cretin, Charlotte of Mecklenburg," she said one day at lunch. I noticed they'd discontinued the use of drinking straws and now expected us all to put our lips directly on the chocolate milk carton's wet and slimy cardboard opening. The menu board, a rusty, lettered display case next to the much-larger case containing athletic trophies and plaques, displayed only one ominous word: "fingers."

"Hi, Joan," I said. "I'm not going to college."

Teachers—and certainly librarians—were expressly forbidden from touching students, but such an arcane rule did not stop Joan from grabbing my earlobe and pulling me into the reference section of the library, officially closed during lunch but now open to her hectoring abuse. "You're a fool, Charlotte, if you think for one second you'll be able to get by in this world without furthering your education," she said. "Be seated until the bell rings; I'm not finished with you yet."

"My parents," I said. "They can't afford—"

"Nonsense," she said. "They own their house don't they?

Just the other day, I saw your mother buying Land O' Lakes butter at Best Yet."

I told her I'd applied for admission and been accepted at both Rogers State and Oklahoma State in Stillwater, but was seriously considering a job stacking bags of fertilizer at Garden Gate south of town. "The pay is good," I said. "Because I'm so strong."

"You're an imbecile," she said. "I know the man who owns Garden Gate, and let's just say he's not one to rack up the library fines, if you know what I mean."

"It's just for the summer," I said. "And maybe into the fall."

She wouldn't hear of it, of course, and before I knew what was happening, I was copying out words from the dictionary and using an ancient field guide to identify the birds on the windowsill outside. She wrote me a pass for my fourth hour Chemistry class, and I outright skipped Calculus and Band. All afternoon she put me to work: shelving periodicals, opening junk mail, looking for outdated borders in an Atlas from the 1970s. And she told me about her past, that she hadn't always been a librarian but once had been a flight attendant out of New York City and dated Paul Anka. Without my even asking, she launched into a long diatribe about her nephews and niece, "The Listless Wonders" she called them, because all three had developed an aversion to vigorous outdoor activity and instead spent all their time watching televised sporting events and talking to their supposed friends on the telephone.

Friends? The Whole Grain Gang, The Listless Wonders, had *friends*? Somehow I'd imagined they were too sheltered—and, as a result, too weird—for friends and instead had no choice but to content themselves with their nerdy and disgusting parents and eccentric and sad old aunt. Or maybe they had goldfish or a turtle. Definitely not dogs or cats.

"That reminds me," she said. "Elliot is taking a campus tour at OSU. His father wants him to go to Penn, of course, but his foolish mother wants him close to home."

"Elliot?" I said. "His name is Elliot?"

"You're going to be late for Calculus," she said. "Mrs. Keener will be annoyed."

"Maybe I *do* want to go to OSU," I said. "I could still work at Garden Gate on weekends."

She told me that if I did decide to attend Oklahoma's fine—though flawed—state university, I'd have no choice but to join the Spirit Band for sure and therefore would have to spend my weekends traveling with the football team, something I would have thought she'd have found beneath the good tastes of someone who'd almost become a National Merit Scholar, but that was Joan: full of surprises. I thought for sure Elliot was in the band at his own high school, probably a trumpet player, or maybe the trombone. I myself played the oboe, and though I'd considered quitting band on many occasions, I suddenly imagined my future in the football stands, my feet propped up on Elliot's trombone case while my fellow woodwind players, envious of my new status as someone's girlfriend, painted a tiny replica of OSU's legendary mascot, Pistol Pete, on my slim and feminine cheek.

The unpleasant, fateful reality was that my campus tour of OSU was not accompanied by Elliot at all but by one of the quilted purse-carrying whole grain gang, not Elliot's mother but his aunt, along with the weirdo blonde girl, Elliot's cousin, I supposed, whose name, it turned out, was Prudence. On the day of the tour—it was a Monday—I saw Joan feeding a crust of bread to a wayward goose at the idyllic campus hotspot they called Theta Pond.

"Where's Elliot?" I said. "I mean, I thought he was thinking about going to OSU."

"Prudence is the real brains of the family," Joan said, tossing a whole piece of bread in the water's murky depths. "She, too, would be better off far away from here, but already she's well-established in the university community."

The whole thing seemed strange—I was missing my chance to become Elliot's girlfriend—and I decided at once the drive from Claremore to Stillwater had been a waste. Prudence, forlorn and fidgety on a park bench at the far end of Theta Pond, appeared neither old enough to go to college nor animated enough to endure the campus tour. Even worse, I would discover, she was a child prodigy, only fourteen and already in possession of her high school diploma, earned not in the public schools but through homeschooling (of course) and the sickly look she had at Cowboy Mall was due to a long-ago case of pinworms. "That's gross," I said to Joan. "I think I'm going to skip out and go home."

"Nonsense," she said. "You and Prudence are going to see the wonders of this fine university while her mother and I chat over cups of coffee in the Student Union. Now go over there and introduce yourself."

I looked over at the wooden bench, positioned inconveniently under a shedding gingko tree, where Prudence remained out of earshot, her hands gripping the railings and her mouth twisted into unmistakable grimace of someone recently chewing on the unsavory strands of her own hair. She did not appear friendly. I noticed a blooming strawberry-colored stain on the collar of her shirt, yesterday's popsicle probably, or cough medicine refused from a spoon.

"I'm Charlotte," I said. "What do you think of OSU?"

"Sucks," she said. "Frat boys and losers."

"You've seen frat boys?"

"They killed a swan," she said. "Its partner died of a broken heart."

"When?"

"Yesterday," she said. "I saw the whole thing."

"They give campus tours on Sundays?"

"Our campus tour is *today*, dipshit; I was here yesterday to work in the lab."

Of course she was employed helping high-dollar faculty members with something important and complex, a top secret project involving code names from the Department of Defense. "Nothing that kills people," she said. "It has to do with gene mutations in cattle." When I asked her to tell me what happened with the fraternity boys and the swan, she began to cry, at first only a suppressed sniffle, and then a great wave of sobs. I sat down beside her on the wooden bench. I'd never been good around crying people. Once, when we were much younger, my sister came home from school with a busted lip. I sent her to the garage to look for hydrogen peroxide and then locked the door behind her. No one noticed her absence until just before dinner, when my mother asked me to set the table and I refused. My sister still described that series of events to strangers, as if to demonstrate some essential flaw in my character. With Prudence, I decided to keep quiet. When her breathing steadied, she told me the story of the swan, the feathers flying, the audible scream, the chorus of drunken laughter, the whole gruesome ordeal, from beginning to tragic end.

"That's terrible," I said. "Those boys should be expelled."

"They should be in jail," she said.

"My uncle's in jail," I said. "He was a thief."

"What did he steal?"

"A car and two horse trailers," I said. "Not at the same time."

"Let's skip the campus tour," she said. "I'll show you my study carrel at the library."

Nothing—aside from possibly the campus tour—sounded more boring than seeing Prudence's study carrel at the library, but I wanted to be a good sport, impress her maybe, so that she would invite me into her world of whole grains and political protest. I'd been to the Rogers State Library before, but the Oklahoma State Library, with its Georgian architecture and fountain out front, was far grander, if a little disappointing once you made it to shabby, narrow stairwell in the middle of the building. Everyone there—librarians, students, and even a custodian—seemed to know Prudence and addressed her by name. "Well, if it isn't Hester Prudence-Prynne," another student, an older-looking woman wearing all black and carrying a tall stack of books, said as we made our way to the fourth floor. Prudence gave her a high-five and asked her about a change in their scheduled lab work; they laughed at some secret shared knowledge of their professor's peculiar eating habits. The sickly cast to her countenance faded, and she walked with occasional skips mixed in, the kind of thing a real college student would be too embarrassed to do, but because she was so smart and only fourteen, people—and I'll admit I was among them—were charmed.

Her study carrel was unremarkable, identical, as it was, to all the rest. When she turned to greet yet another friendly library patron, I looked at the plastic folders she had neatly stacked in a tray and saw on the carrel's side panel she had Scotch-taped a single fortune cookie message, "your fondest wish will come true." I knew this was my opportunity to ask about her fondest wish and whether or not it already had come true, but before I could find a clever way to phrase the question, she edged me out of the way and sat down in the carrel's plastic chair.

"Let's work," she said. "Go find yourself a book to read. Pick something from the *Nonfiction* section, a subject you've never before encountered, and begin."

I could see she had much in common with her Aunt Joan. Something about the way she placed her newly-sharpened number two pencils squarely on the desktop also reminded me of my sister, older than Prudence in years, but far younger in terms of overall wisdom. I followed her instructions and picked a book about bodies of water in Massachusetts, somewhere I'd never been. It seemed to me Oklahoma probably did not have enough notable bodies of water to merit their own book, and, because I'd read *Walden* the year before, I thought I'd find some unexpected insight from reading about Mary's Pond or Leonard's Pond, both places I was sure remained rooted in the unspeakable beauty and solitude of prior centuries. The book, of course, was a disappointment, full of depth charts and dry descriptions of calcium hardness and total alkalinity. When I looked up, Prudence was gone.

Again I looked at the fortune cookie message: "your fondest wish will come true." It seemed to me a person like Prudence could not have a fondest wish, if only because the scope of her imagination was limited to library books and her low-level work in the lab. The OSU students were nice to her, sure, but were they really her friends? She didn't even have a driver's license.

It occurred to me I did not know my way back to Theta Pond, and I'd never even seen the Student Union. Perhaps I was no better than Prudence, a mere child at an adult university. I read a few more pages of *Bodies of Water of the Commonwealth of Massachusetts* before checking both fourth floor restrooms, only to find them empty. I asked at the circulation desk if anyone had seen a young girl with stringy blond hair, and the librarian, a man who looked exactly like Albert Einstein save for the nametag on the pocket of his collared shirt that said "Evan Farber," said, "You mean Prudence?"

"Yes," I said. "You know her too."

"Of course," he said. "She's probably in the fountain out front. Dress rehearsal."

Indeed she was a true renaissance woman because in addition to her advanced abilities in the sciences and her keen political instincts inherited from her aunt, she was a gifted actress, starring as Xanthius in a production of Aristophanes' *The Frogs*. Evan Farber ushered me down the library's front steps, where I watched from the landing as she leaped from the low wall surrounding the fountain and onto the back of a tall guy with terrible acne, Dionysus, I assumed, though he might have been Pluto or an unnamed slave. I didn't want to interrupt the dress rehearsal, but I wondered why she hadn't told me about it before.

I suppose I should not have been alarmed by the appearance of people dressed as frogs during dress rehearsal for a production of *The Frogs.* "Brek-ek-ek-ek-ex, ko-ax, ko-ax," they said in unison. "Welcome to the Fountain and the Lake; Let us wake!"

"Stop," the director said. "Take five," which turned into ten, which turned into fifteen, every minute another excuse for Prudence to introduce me to another member of the cast. "My cool new friend from Claremore," she called me, which, even though she was only fourteen and in some ways embarrassing, made me feel important in a way I'd never felt at home.

Prudence, it turned out, was a smoker, and after that afternoon I became one myself. On the library lawn, the world was free and easy, and we found ourselves eluding our scheduled meet-up time with her mother and Joan. I knew I should be asking about her handsome and irreverent cousin Elliot, but I was having so much fun I lost interest.

"Charlotte's a Capricorn," Prudence said to a student wearing frog goggles. "So you can trust her."

I had not told her my birthday, but I remembered she'd asked to see my driver's license on the walk from Theta Pond. "What would you do," I said. "If your fondest wish really *did* come true?"

"Take a bow," she said. "Blow kisses to the crowd."

"Sure," I said. "As if."

The frogs gathered in a huddle in the fountain's cloudy water while Prudence strutted down the sidewalk, her arms outstretched in a grand demonstration of what I realized was her regal beauty. Watching the rehearsal, I was reminded of a book I'd read about the early days of vaudeville, that vocation and vacation could be one and the same. Prudence and her actor friends seemed otherworldly somehow, not at all like the people I knew in Claremore, and after about ten minutes in their company I realized I had no choice but to go to Oklahoma State and major in Theatre. People can be glib about those moments in life that prove influential only after many years of reflection, but indeed this was one of those moments, and although I did, in fact, major in Theatre, and did, in fact, enjoy a brief stint as a professional stage manager so far off-Broadway it might as well have been Claremore's Main Street, I later went back to school and became something else entirely. Nowadays, when my life becomes boring, I look back on that summer I spent with Prudence, and—sometimes—wonder what became of her. Every year on her birthday, I look her up on Facebook and Twitter, and last year I even paid one of those huckster services twenty-two dollars to try to find her current address, but ultimately I had no luck. (Women: do not take your husband's name when you marry. If you're fortunate enough to marry a woman, do not take her name, either). Joan died long ago. Elliot's life as a seller of high-end speedboats shows up on Instagram, but somehow I've never wanted to contact him. He turned out ugly, for one thing, and not because of his looks.

At home, my father, who'd been demoted to the stock room at JC Penney, expressed his daily annoyance I was considering college at all. A couple of years would pass before he left my mother for the principal's secretary; that last summer at home his pretense of devotion to my mother was still intact, his fatherly advice still dispensed with ease. Every day he told me he thought I had a good chance at Assistant Manager at Garden Gate, and the bonus, he said, was that I could keep my mornings free to help out my mother at the barn. But I wanted to move to Stillwater, and although I kept it a secret until just days before my departure, nothing, not even the threat of living without my parents' love, would stop me.

That spring, my sister, who'd grown egotistical since becoming third runner-up in the Wrestling Homecoming Court, also became Student Council Treasurer and, though she wasn't an athlete, the "Outreach Coordinator" for the Fellowship of Christian Athletes. Prudence and I had taken to calling it "The Fellatio of Christian Fatsoes," but—to be fair—my sister wasn't fat.

One morning—I remember: it was the Friday designated "Senior Skip Day"—I decided to visit Joan in the library before First Hour. Like most seniors, I had decided against skipping class; it seemed like too much trouble somehow, since I had two semester tests and I knew my unexcused absence would mean the principal's secretary would call my mother for sure. But Prudence—oh the luck of the home-schooled!—took every day off and wanted me to skip fifth and sixth periods at least so that I could drive her to a Janet Jackson concert at the Myriad Convention Center in Oklahoma City. She'd wanted to arrive early, to bring lawn chairs to stake out our places in line. I'd refused, citing my "real world" responsibilities at school, but I knew she'd find a way to go without me. She'd had the whole thing planned for months, buying combat boots from the army surplus store and clip-on earrings from the mall.

"Well, if it isn't The Lady of Shalott," Joan said that morning at the library. "Studying hard on Senior Skip Day."

"Calculus," I said. "I made a C on the last test."

"Appropriate," she said. "A worthless subject by all accounts."

"I'm going to college," I said. "Don't worry."

"Only cretins go to *college*," she said. "You must learn to call it *university*."

"I'm going to university," I said. "Even if I have to pay for it myself."

She told me about a series of scholarships given away by local businesses; I was relieved JC Penney was not among them. When I assured her I would apply for every available opportunity for financial aid, she left me alone for a while and busied herself shelving books and pushing chairs under tables. I remember she was coughing a lot and seemed unsteady on her feet. I'd studied enough from my calculus textbook I knew I could at least pass my upcoming exam, but something changed when the bell rang and I began to shovel my books into my backpack.

"I think you should skip this foolish exercise in rote memory," she said. "A certain niece of mine requires your company at a certain Janet Jackson concert."

There, suddenly, like the man behind the curtain in *The Wizard of Oz*, Prudence appeared from the depths of the reference section and tossed Joan's car keys at my head. I wasn't quick enough to catch them.

"Here," she said. "Aunt Joan said we could take her Cutlass."

"I have a test."

"I have boots your size in the back seat," she said. "Come on."

I looked out the library's front door where I could see students slamming locker doors, making last-dash trips to the water fountains and restrooms, finally leaving the halls in silence as they shuffled off to class. The world would not come to an end if I missed my Calculus exam; in fact, I easily could have faked an illness and pulled off my own Okie version of *Ferris Bueller's Day Off*, but—and here was the tragic part—I *wanted* to take that test, and I wanted to do well. I told her I'd think about it, *weigh my options*, I said, as we walked out to the faculty parking lot.

On the other side of the cafeteria dumpsters was a hedgerow, and on the other side of the hedgerow was a row of air conditioning units, and on the other side of the air conditioning units was a flagpole, and at the base of the flagpole was my twin sister, folding the stars and stripes not with the help of another person, not in the proper, deliberate way that honors the tri-cornered hat worn by the colonial soldiers during the war for Independence, but in the same, haphazard way a harried housewife, alone after everyone has gone off to school or work, might crumple a fitted sheet into a ball and shove it into the linen closet without washing it first. That morning she'd left the house early, an extra-curricular event, she said, though she insisted in sentences rapid and breathless that neither the principal nor his secretary should have been so rigid in enforcing some silly, outdated rules about the separation of Church and State.

"That's right," my mother had said. "They're trying to keep our kids away from God."

"Not Sheila," said my father. That was the name of the principal's secretary. "I know she's good with God."

The event, it turned out, was called *See You at the Pole*, and it was sweeping the nation, first Fort Worth, then Dallas, Oklahoma City, and finally our own Claremore High School, where the Fellowship of Christian Athletes urged all students who walked in the way of the lord to spend every Friday morning before the bell rang gathered around the flagpole in prayer.

"Oh god," my sister said when she saw me. "It's you."

"*Fellatio*," Prudence whispered in my ear. "*Fatsoes.*"

"I forgot my Calculus book," I said. "I think I might have dropped it in the parking lot."

"It's in your hand," my sister said.

"My other Calculus book," I said. "The workbook."

"Just leave me alone, Charlotte," she said. "Take that prune-faced, devil-worshipping friend of yours and skip off to an Ozzy Osbourne concert or something, okay-? I hope he eats the head off a puppy and you can feel *great* about yourself."

"She doesn't worship the devil," I said.

"I don't even *like* Ozzy Osbourne," Prudence said.

"Look," my sister said. "I know what you think of me. That I'm *boring*. That I'm *delusional*. That I *disapprove* of you and your stupid college friends who don't even study anything *real*." She shoved the crumpled flag under her arm and tried to hide it from view. "But I prayed for you, Charlotte. I prayed for your *soul*."

"Amen," Prudence said. "Hallelujah."

"How dare you mock me," my sister said. "You're not even old enough to *own* a bible, much less *read* one."

"I'm old enough to kick your ass," Prudence said.

"Hold on," I said.

"I dare you," my sister said. "Come at me, smoker-girl. Black lung. Cancer queen."

"Is that the best you can do?" Prudence said.

"Pinworms," my sister said. "Scabies. Scurvy. *Venereal Disease.*"

"Who told you I had pinworms?" Prudence said. "Thanks a lot, Charlotte."

"Wait a second," I said. I turned to my sister and wrestled the flag from her grip. "What happened here? Shouldn't you be in class by now?"

Her shoulders fell as she told me only three other students had shown up for *See You at the Pole*—an eighth grade girl everyone knew was not allowed to wear pants, the Student Council President who dutifully attended all school-sponsored events, and a Swedish exchange student who wanted to learn the weird ways of American culture. The tape recorder she'd borrowed from our church had dead batteries and no one had even thought to bring a bible.

"Why would you even need a tape recorder to *pray?*" Prudence said. "That's stupid."

"It's for the music, dumbass," my sister said. "To get you in the mood."

Impulsively, I threw the flag to the ground; my sister actually gasped—she gasped!—and scooped it up immediately, brushed leaves from the fabric, and began again her fruitless attempts to crease the edges into a triangle.

"You could learn some respect, Charlotte," she said. "The Founding Fathers are watching."

"Your own father doesn't give a shit," I said.

"He's tired," she said. "You could try taking his side for once."

I knew then I'd be missing both my Calculus exam and the Janet Jackson concert, that I'd join the long tradition of seniors actually skipping on Senior Skip Day and take Prudence for a spin somewhere, maybe to Stillwater to see our theater friends, maybe to the library or the lake. For it was that day I became something like a person in charge of my own destiny, and though Prudence was obsessed with Janet Jackson I refused to take her to the concert, and though my better instincts told me to remain at school, I silenced those as well, and though my sister told a lie, perhaps the first official lie of her life, when she went home that day and told my parents I was staying late to shelve books with Joan, I came home only once more at all, to pack up my belongings and carry them in haste to Joan's coughing Cutlass, after which we would make the drive to *university*, to term-papers and takeout, the beginning of what would become the rest of my life.

The Old-Fashioned Way

Ross was the type of guy one hoped never to run into at the grocery store because of his big, fat mouth. Really, he was not that fat; instead I would have characterized him as tall and hefty, like the magnolia tree he cut down in his side yard, only without the possibility of blossom. Back then he was just my neighbor, father to twin teenagers Allison and Ralph, and the wood shop teacher at the local high school, which might have led you to believe he kept up his property by painting the shutters, polishing the porch railings, or building birdhouses complete with turrets, terraces, and a colonnade. He did none of these things. Instead, he mowed his postage-stamp-sized lawn—on a riding lawn mover!—over and over again, even during periods of extreme drought. Allison and Ralph just stood there in their Bermuda shorts and preppy, collared shirts, checking their phones for scheduled appointments for tennis lessons or skin care consultations. All this might have led you to believe I lived in a fancy, gated community, but I did not. Allison and Ralph were fakers, just like their father, and we lived in a solidly middle class neighborhood right behind the hospital, where I worked in respiratory therapy. I thought I'd like to give Ross an asthma attack, though I didn't know for sure he even had asthma, but if he did have it I hoped all that lawn mowing made him suffer and wheeze.

One year on the Fourth of July—Allison and Ralph were visiting their mother in a faraway state—Ross invited me over for hotdogs. He said it like that, too. "How about a hotdog, Harriet? To celebrate our Founding Fathers? Fireworks start at dark." I should clarify that Ross once called me, "Mrs. Fast," and only started referring to me as Harriet after my husband died in a boating accident, not that I ever confided in Ross or asked him to call me Harriet or even told him about the boating accident, but it was a small town, and people took advantage. I should clarify, too, that I had no plans for the Fourth of July.

"No thanks," I said. "I have plans."

"Suit yourself," he said. "But if you change your mind—"

"Not a big hot dog fan," I said. "Thanks."

He went on to say he'd be adding hot Italian sausages and tofu pups, along with cocktails and an array of side dishes, including his mother's famous Jell-O salad with carrots and raisins. Some other neighbors would be coming by, he said, along with a group of his students from Summer Driver's Ed, and my presence would be a welcomed distraction from the anticipated argument between Katie, a Driver's Ed student, and Nancy, the neighbor who owned a hair salon a couple of blocks over—something about a set of expensive hair extensions that turned out to be synthetic, he said, though he didn't like to meddle in other people's affairs.

I once again demurred and imagined myself hiding in the dark depths of my bedroom, watching a bad movie or turning in early. I decided to take a chance. "Maybe I'll stop by," I said. "Thank you for thinking of me."

"I'm always thinking of you, Harriet," he said. "I mean, sometimes."

I mistakenly imagined this last remark was little more than commonplace neighborly decorum, for I'd forgotten how to flirt and maybe—let's be honest—never really knew how to talk to men to begin with. My husband, before his untimely death, had been a scrub tech in the OR, and our first, last, and only date had been over dubiously manufactured nachos in the hospital's snack bar. You may be wondering how a common scrub tech and a respiratory therapist were able to afford a boat and therefore end up in a fatal boating accident. Well, it wasn't our boat. It belonged to my husband's grandfather, Pops, they called him, and even though he and I shared the same birthday, he never liked me and in fact would not allow me on his boat. Pops, of course, came away from the boating accident completely unscathed. To this day I think of him on our shared birthday and wonder if he's alive or dead.

On the morning of the Fourth of July, I made the mistake of calling Ross to ask him whether or not he needed me to bring anything to the party.

"Are you a vegan?" he said. "Because I hate vegans."

"No," I said. "But it's pretty common these days."

"Are you allergic to anything?" he said. "Any particular

scents that bother you?"

"Nope," I said. "I mean, there are certain scents that are universally loathed."

"Yeah, like lotion," he said. "I hate lotion."

"Look, do you want me to bring anything or not?"

"Don't bring lotion," he said. "Whatever you do."

These peculiarities—the constant lawn mowing and the lotion hatred—were merely the first two entries on a long list of unfortunate character traits, oddities I would discover and rediscover over a period of years. On that particular Fourth of July, I threw caution to the wind and brought along a six-pack of Canadian beer, as I did not want to appear too patriotic, another mistake, I realized later, when Ross hugged me and said his favorite sport was hockey and Allison and Ralph both ordered their acne medications from an online Canadian pharmacy.

"Wonderful," I said. "I'll bet they save a lot of money that way."

"You have no idea," he said. "The zits."

The promised feud between the Driver's Ed student and the hairdresser did not come to pass, but another set of neighbors, the Hornburgers, who were otherwise very nice if a little hard of hearing, set off a firestorm when they complained of unspecified people leaving "wet trash" in unsealed bags on the curbside, therefore attracting raccoons.

"If it's not *your* house, who the hell cares?" Ross said.

"But it *is* my house," Mr. Hornburger said. "It's all our houses."

"I'm not too worried about it," I said, and that was it: the beginning of the end. Damn it all, reader, I married him. I didn't want to, but I did. I mean, it was a second marriage for both of us, so it hardly counted as anything important. And the time that elapsed between that Fourth of July party and our wedding ceremony on the loading dock at the local high school was a mere six weeks-! Can you believe such a thing? That's how much of a sucker I was, how much I hated those nights spent alone in the company of my mediocre memories of my long-dead husband: six weeks of wooing that consisted of little more than a weekend trip to Eureka Springs and a couple of movie dates at the Satellite Twin. And Ralph and Allison hated me, almost as much as Pops before them had hated me, though Allison eventually came around to borrowing my makeup and telling me I looked pretty in strapless gowns, not that I wore strapless gowns very often, but she seemed to approve whenever I did. That's how the whole thing at the grocery store happened—the thing where I told Ross he had a big, fat mouth. Little did I know the principal of the local high school overheard the whole conversation from the gluten-free section.

"Oh my god, Harriet," Ross said in the ketchup aisle. I was actually buying barbecue sauce. This was long after our courtship and well into the four long years of our marriage. I'd stopped at the store after work and didn't expect to run into him there. He was holding a block of cheddar cheese— the cheap kind—and a can of Pringles Lite. Also, he was sweaty from mowing the lawn.

"Hi honey," I said. "I guess I'll see you at home. Do you think Ralph and Allison will want some lunch meat?"

"Why in the *world* would you wear a *sleeveless evening gown* to the grocery store?" he said. "Someone will see."

"This is not an evening gown," I said. "And I wore it to work."

"You wore it to *work*?" he said. "At the *hospital*?"

"Yeah," I said. "I mean, I brought a sweater."

"You cannot cover your filth with a mere sweater," he said.

You see what I mean about his big, fat mouth? I wasn't kidding before. People like to talk about meeting romantic partners the old-fashioned way, as if there's something inherently good and decent about borrowing a cup of sugar or attending an impromptu barbecue on the Fourth of July, but at that moment in the grocery store, I knew I'd have settled for one of those online creepazoids any day if it meant I'd never again have to hear the fateful sound of the riding lawn mower's low rumble. And it's a good thing the principal of the high school overheard us that day; otherwise the divorce settlement might have gone south for sure. Ross was a lawn-mowing, lotion-hating, modesty-loving shop teacher who tried to sleep with one of his Driver's Ed students. (More on that last part later). People generally don't believe women about these things, but they're true.

On the Lookout for Nazis These Days

The neighbor's dog was named Ruby, and she was a good dog, I thought, even when she had a guilty look in her eye and feathers hanging from her mouth. Her owner—Zeke was his name—said she was royalty, bred from the finest Rhodesian Ridgeback lines on the planet. A Rodeo Wetback, he called her, *My Little Pepita*. But all the neighbors called her Ruby the Killer: her daily escape from Zeke's yard spelled trouble for Cara's chickens, and even a call to the local animal control office would not keep Ruby from stalking the neighborhood for the smell of blood. All that would have been fine—another more or less predictable turn in the slow news cycle of rural Oklahoma life—were it not for Zeke carrying his goddamned gun everywhere he went. Ever since he'd put a confederate flag sticker on the back window of his pickup I'd been on the lookout for additional signs of trouble—cars I'd never seen before parked in his yard, bonfires at odd hours, tall stacks of pizza boxes left for the raccoons. Cara said he was a good boy, kind to strangers of all walks of life, and I shouldn't worry. But Cara had made mistakes before.

"He doesn't go to church," she said. "I've seen him making doughnut runs on Sunday mornings."

Usually I ran into Cara at the feed store or grocery store or most often the drug store. This time I was at the bank, hilarious if you thought about it because none of us in that crappy town had any money to speak of. I was there with my old man, not my husband or father, but the old man I took care of for money. Not very much money. The bank was hosting some kind of fake celebration that day, balloons and streamers decorating the lobby, giveaway Frisbees for children under twelve. My old man wanted to make a withdrawal. Earlier, in the car, he'd wanted to use his walker, but I'd insisted on the wheelchair instead. Dragging that thing in and out of the back seat just about killed my back, but it was a lot faster than watching him take two steps every half hour. But he couldn't help it. He was old.

"Every weekday morning, that boy's up at the crack of dawn," Cara said. "He's hardworking."

"Where does he work these days?" I said. My old man was coughing up a storm.

"He's working for Coca-Cola," she said. "Drives a truck."

"And he needs a gun for that?"

"Maybe," she said. "You'll have to ask him."

Zeke had been my neighbor for five or six years at least, ever since his parents kicked him out of their doublewide and he set out on his own. I made a point not to speak to him if I could help it, but our houses were close enough I could hear him run the vacuum cleaner, something he did periodically but not reliably, usually on mornings when I wanted to sleep in. He had a new truck every six months, leased, I thought, not bought. His parents still paid for everything, I was pretty sure. Cara knew all these people better than I did. And she spied on them. Probably she spied on me more than I even knew. Lately I was gone all the time, doing my mail route in the mornings and taking care of my old man in the afternoons. Sometimes I went to Stillwater to see a movie or get some chicken wings. Not very often.

"His brother works for the city," Cara said. "They're decent."

You might think everyone in Perkins, Oklahoma was a card-carrying member of the NRA, but you'd be wrong. Cara and I were reliable Democrats, atheists, pro-choice, pro-immigration, and—you would not think this last part would be controversial—against gun nuts and their threat to public safety. My old man, too, was a Democrat, though he kept his politics a secret from everyone but me. But Cara and I were vocal, in our way. In her former life, Cara had been a schoolteacher—she taught "Business Ethics" at the Junior High—so she came by her political leanings by virtue of her lousy paycheck and ever-increasing class sizes. I, on the other hand, was a throwback, raised in the Woody Guthrie tradition of labor-left activists and fellow travelers: *"No, no, Old Man Trump!"* Cara lost her job when the school districts consolidated, and my lefty parents were long dead; still, we kept the home fires burning.

Why she always spoke highly of this right-wing kid, Zeke, I didn't know. I could account for some of her misplaced (idiotic) loyalty by virtue of the fact that Zeke's dad was her uncle's best friend. Really, though, why did I bother to think about Zeke at all? He was annoying, sure, and certainly one had to be on the lookout for Nazis these days. But the year before I'd seen him in a Bernie Sanders T-shirt, so I'll admit I was confused. He was impressionable, I figured, a slave to fashion, and the Confederate flag sticker was small, not the actual flag but something similar, with a catchy phrase about the clean air in Arkansas in large letters below. His people were Okies as far as I knew.

"These nutcase kids aren't all religious," I said. My old man nodded. "Sometimes they're just *radicalized online*, you know."

"He's a nice kid," Cara said. "I just know it."

We argued back and forth for a while about his dog killing her chickens, about the new bloodstains in his yard from freshly-killed game, about his uncritical display of white supremacist symbols. All the while she defended him, obviously trying to make him seem better than he was.

I pushed my old man back toward the bank's front entrance. Cara stayed behind at the giveaway table. I looked ahead and saw what I thought was a stranger removing his hat and bowing in the direction of me and my old man. I watched as he held the door open with only his index finger, as if to indicate the door was very light or he was very strong. All the young men in Perkins looked more or less the same—ball caps and chewing tobacco and blue jeans—but as I pushed my old man closer and the stranger scratched his forehead, I realized this particular stranger was Zeke. I noticed right away he was without his gun—for once. My old man was counting the money from his withdrawal.

"Don't count your dolphins before they hatch," Zeke said to my old man.

"Good one," my old man said. "Dolphins."

"Erin," Zeke said to me. "Have you been keeping my *Sports Illustrated*?"

"I'm not on your route any more," I said. "Dumbass."

"Language," he said. "Public service employees should be setting a good example for today's youth."

"You're not a kid anymore, Zeke."

"That's right," he said. "I'm grown."

My old man looked up from his wad of cash. "I remember your dad," he said. "He was a hoodlum."

Just then, Cara was upon us. She shoved a stack of Frisbees in my old man's lap. "Who was a hoodlum?" she said. "I want to know."

"No one," I said.

"Zeke's dad," my old man said. "He stole a retarded girl's cat. When he was young."

"Which retarded girl?" Cara said. "I don't know any retarded girls."

"They moved," my old man said. "Partly because they were upset about their cat."

"My dad never stole no retarded girl's cat," Zeke said.

"I'm sure he didn't," Cara said. "He was on the school board."

By then my old man had pocketed his wad of cash and thrown the Frisbees on the floor. A security guard keeping watch over the vault was giving us all the eye. I wanted out of there—and I knew it was past my old man's lunch time—so I told Cara I'd meet her for coffee later on. I watched as Zeke, his ball cap pushed over his eyes, slouched back to Coca-Cola truck, which I, noticed, he'd left unlocked. I was sure his gun was in there somewhere. Probably it was loaded. Probably he'd never think of pointing it at another person, but I couldn't be sure. Probably Cara was right, and he was a nice boy, deep down.

My old man wanted to stop at McDonald's. He bought me a soft-serve and we sat on the playground a while, the two of us keeping company with runny-nosed children feeding French fries to the birds. The whole thing was supposed to seem charming, but I was not charmed. Work is work, and even though I liked my old man, I was tired of his company. He didn't talk much, for one thing, and when he did he wanted only to talk about the past, usually the distant past. I'm not too far from old age myself, so I try to guard against false nostalgia. The self-help books tell you to *live in the moment*, and I believed in that kind of thing, for a while. My old man hated McDonald's. I don't know why he always wanted to go there.

When I got home that night, Zeke's truck was nowhere to be seen, and Ruby was chained in the front yard. She wasn't barking, not at first, but I could see that sleepy look in her eye and feathers hanging from her mouth. Cara had lost two chickens the week before. She'd added another layer of fence panels to her coop, but they'd been no match for Ruby. Why Cara thought maintaining good relations with some no-account kid was more important than her own damned chickens I didn't know. It's true those chickens were replaceable in her eyes. She liked having the eggs, but didn't want to slaughter the chickens herself and so "sent them away" to a different set of neighbors after they stopped laying. Everyone around that crappy town had similar pretensions to the fake life of fake frontiersmen. People set up shelters full of canned goods and rusty canteens full of water—not because they needed them but because the set-up itself was a kind of hobby, like collecting deer skulls or stretching skins across your garage. Everyone wanted to appear hard-nosed and proud, as if they could, if they needed to, live off the land. The truth was they liked their Frito-chili-pies and video games and reality TV and would not give them up for the world.

Since I knew Zeke was gone and Ruby wouldn't hurt me as long as she was chained, I decided to sidle along the edges of his property for a closer look. At first I saw nothing unusual: tipped-over lawn chairs, trash bags unmoored from their cans, firewood stacked sloppily against the back fence. He did not keep things altogether tidy. Last year's potted plants lay like forgotten relics at the base of his stairs, and bumper stickers urging people to *Eat Beef* and *Live Simply so that others may Simply Live* peeled from the tin-roofed lean-to housing his collection of hockey sticks, baseball bats, miscellaneous sections of PVC, fishing rods, post-hole diggers, weed-trimmers, and rakes. He did not appear to live all that simply, but what did I care? Then I saw something unusual: a pile of fake flowers, their stems caked with unmistakable signs of dried hot glue, had blown into a corner of the front porch. Underneath them was a hand-lettered sign: *Just Married—Zeke and Lindsay Claire.*

Just then, Ruby caught sight of me and started to sound the alarm, at first a quick series of barks, then a low, long howl. I made my way through the thicket of pokeweed and honeysuckle separating my property line from Zeke's, all the while my phone in my hand so that I could text under the light of the moon.

Zeke got married. I wrote to Cara. *To someone named Lindsay Claire.*

I know. Cara replied. *I went to the wedding. Gave them an Arby's gift card, ha.*

I'll admit I was annoyed she hadn't told me before. Cara was keyed into all the latest evidence of small town ceremony, and she thought she had everyone fooled into thinking she was some kind of junior leaguer or country club maven; she even made donations to stupid stuff like Save the Statues and Help the Mayor Pay for his Educational Trip to Mount Rushmore (when really he has enough money to pay for it himself). She thought she had everyone sold on the fact of her altruism and civic pride, but everyone knew she was a phony and kept up appearances only for the sake of her side business leasing plots of her grandfather's land to squatters in search of a better life, usually undocumented migrant workers down on their luck. Turned out Zeke's new bride was herself the child of migrant workers; they were from Guatemala, Cara said, but they looked white. But the girl— even whiter still, Cara had the bad taste to mention—was a citizen, born in North Carolina. The girls' parents had been Cara's tenants once upon a time, even parked their double-wide on the edge of her property. Cara said that ever since she re-upped her annual donation to the Daddy Daughter

Dance Refreshments Fund, no one had said a word about her various tenants, all of them hardworking she said, people who kept their heads down and their hands in their pockets. What she was doing with all those donations was obvious bribery, a way to keep her fellow citizens from turning her into the authorities, but no one really talked about it that way. Still, she considered herself upstanding, and I went along for the ride.

"How come no one told me he was getting married?" I said, later over coffee at The Cowboy Cup. "No one cares what I think, I guess."

"They knew you wouldn't come," she said. "To the wedding, I mean."

"It's probably for the best," I said. "Maybe he'll stop carrying that goddamned gun everywhere he goes. *The feminine influence.*"

"She's a hunter too," she said. "All the girls hunt these days. It's A Thing."

"You know her?" I said. "You've *met* her?"

"Sure," she said. "She's cute."

"Cute like psoriasis is cute?"

"No," she said. "Nothing like that. You should get out more, Erin."

I pointed out that I was "out" right at that very moment, drinking a very civilized cup of coffee, with her. She said that didn't count because I was still dressed in my postal uniform, or the shirt with the patch on the shoulder, at least, since I didn't bother with the official scratchy woolen pants. The post office was going to provide me with a fairly comfortable retirement, something Cara and her continuous evasion of federal tax laws could not rightly claim. Plus, she had an Oxy habit everyone in town knew about. Her doctor was a criminal—both in the sense he prescribed just about anything to just about anyone and also in the sense he once used someone else's credit card number to buy a bunch of baseball cards online. Cara had told me all this, of course. She had a backup plan for pills in case he ever went to jail.

"Does she have a job?" I said. "Do you think they'll move?"

"Nursing school," she said. "She's smart."

I figured once she graduated she could get another job just about anywhere, they'd skip town sooner rather than later, and maybe I'd be able to scrape together enough money to buy Zeke's property, have his house bulldozed, plant myself the world's best garden, make a killing at the farmer's market, quit my job caring for my old man, and end up with a better life, what was left of it anyway. I decided right then I'd bring them a plate of cookies—at some point in the future, of course, when I felt like baking cookies. Maybe I'd buy some from the grocery store's bakery.

I drained the rest of my coffee and searched my purse for loose change. Cara spent a lot time talking about illness and death, not unusual, and we each bought another cup of coffee to go. I had my route early the next morning, and she had another doctor's appointment, this one in Oklahoma City, for her back, she said, because it was acting up again. Cara really was my only friend. When she wasn't nodding off she was funny and cool.

That night, just as I turned off the television and headed into the bathroom to brush my teeth, I heard Zeke and his new wife arguing over the sound of their vacuum cleaner. And there was music, too, some kind of rockabilly classic I'd heard years ago at the Tumbleweed Dance Hall south of town. (Don't ask me why I was there; I'm pretty sure it was a friend's baby shower). Anyway, they were shouting, louder than the music, louder than the vacuum cleaner, and Ruby was barking from the yard. I couldn't tell exactly what they were saying, but I made out the words *library, microwave,* and *veterinarian.*

"You're always_____ library," Zeke said.

"_____ microwave," his wife said.

Ruby howled along with the rockabilly song. Zeke must have thought she belonged with the veterinarian because I also made out the word *bitch* and that's when the vacuum cleaner sound stopped abruptly and a door slammed in the echoes of the night. I was dying to know more, so that I'd have something to tell Cara, sure, but also so that I'd have a clearer sense as to when she might be finishing nursing school and ready for gainful employment elsewhere. I thought about stepping outside, but I was sure they'd see me standing in my bathrobe out there in the moonlight. And as I was standing there at the open window, something crossed my mind that almost never did: I'd have to kill him. Someday I might have to kill Zeke. I didn't have my own gun—and really I didn't want one, even living out there in the sticks with the coyotes and bobcats and snakes—but I'd have to find some other way to kill him, poisoned cookies perhaps, or a burning brush pile grown out of control. If they didn't move out within the next six months, if I saw him around town carrying around that goddamned gun, if I saw Klansmen or neo-Nazis gathered for Bible study through the crooked mini-blinds of his living room, if Ruby killed just one more of Cara's chickens, I'd have to kill him, not because anyone needed immediate rescue but because of the simple fact I wanted him dead.

My phone going off in the other room interrupted my murderous thoughts—strange because my phone almost never rang unless it was the Democrats asking for money. This time it was my old man, who said he was having a heart attack. I told him to take two aspirin, unlock his front door, and wait for the paramedics, but he was panicky, afraid he'd fall down before reaching the medicine cabinet. I finally calmed him down enough to convince him to hang up, but when I dialed 9-1-1, the dispatcher didn't believe me.

"This is an *emergency* line," she said. "What *exactly* is your emergency?"

I gave her my old man's address and told her he was having a heart attack.

"Is this man your *husband*?" she said. "Your *father*?"

When I told her I was his care-giver, she said, "Hair-giver?"

I decided to drive over to my old man's house and take him to the hospital myself. I had my keys in the ignition and was about to start the car when the dispatcher finally admitted she'd already sent the ambulance. "I thought he should have someone *with him*," she said. "Because I *care* about the wellbeing of our citizens." After that I made the wise decision to hang up.

Turned out my old man was not having a heart attack at all but was instead suffering from a bad case of food poisoning, and although we could only guess at the culprit, we agreed the French fries at McDonald's had tasted wrong, as if they'd been defrosted in a warm shoebox before frying. And because I felt a little queasy myself, I camped out on his sofa after the long night in the Emergency Room. The next morning, groggy and nauseous, I told my old man I'd have to go home for a shower before heading to the post office for my route.

"That's OK," he said. "I'll call Lindsay Claire."

"As in—Zeke's new wife, Lindsay Claire?"

"She's a nursing student," he said. "Real bright."

"You know her?"

"Sure," he said. "She takes me to McDonald's. Anytime I want."

This was all news to me. Aside from his son, who brought by groceries every week and took him to doctors' appointments and the occasional movie starring Goldie Hawn, I'd had my old man and his empty house pretty much to myself for years. I felt betrayed.

"How long has this been happening?" I said, later, as I was pouring his orange juice and trying to appear cheerful. "This new girl on duty."

"She's strictly volunteer," he said. "She comes over to help me because God told her to."

"And you allow that?"

"Sure," he said. "Why not?"

"Because she'll make you pay her back somehow. In lip service to her church or canned goods or some of your old clothing or something. Nothing is really free these days, not even cheap smiles and charity."

"She's a nice girl," he said. "She doesn't lecture me for one thing."

"She ever talk about Zeke?" I said. "You think they might move?"

"Who's Zeke?" he said. He'd already finished his orange juice and was asking for more. "The kid from the bank? His father was a hoodlum."

"Right," I said. "We've been over that."

Finally convinced I couldn't get any more out of him, I left him to clean up his breakfast dishes on his own and headed to the post office. I was wearing yesterday's clothes and a jacket I'd borrowed from my old man, but no one noticed anything amiss—postal workers in general are not a fashion-loving lot. After I finished sorting and was ready for my route, I texted Cara:

Zeke's wife is a Christian, I wrote. *Like, a Super-Christian.*

For a long time she didn't reply. I figured she was still asleep, sprawled on the sofa in front of the electronica of morning game shows and the muttering of her African Gray. In the middle of my route she finally wrote back:

Duh.

That's all she said. *Duh.* I texted back—at first a series of question marks, then a couple of detailed questions trying to figure out where she was getting her information, but she was incommunicado, gone, I would discover, on radio silence for the entire rest of the week. With anyone else I might have worried, but Cara was like that: friendly one day, more or less absent the next. I figured the game shows were getting good or she needed some more sleep. In any case, I let it go, figured she'd been digging through their garbage cans and found a church bulletin at the bottom. People told her stuff they wouldn't tell me. In my case I was bothered, by being supplanted at my old man's house, yes, but also by the prospect of Zeke—whom we'd always known to be more or less apathetic and lazy on Sunday mornings—converting to a full-scale commitment to Love Thy Neighbor. When you thought of all the townspeople more or less bleeding the blood of the lamb it seemed like no big deal, another drop in the bucket of what always happened when Jesus wept, but the confederate flag sticker had me worried: what if they came after me?

The last thing I expected was to see Cara standing in Zeke's front yard when I pulled into my driveway one afternoon, but there she was, holding her phone even, waving frantically at the ambulance blaring sirens behind me in the distance. She was distraught—tears running down her face, hair all crazy in the wind—and I realized right away that something terrible had happened, something heart-stopping, something that surely would show up in the newspaper the next day and the next day and the day after that. I rolled down my driver's side window.

Zeke's dog Ruby was dead in the front yard.

"My little Pepita," Zeke said, hugging her lifeless body to his chest. "I killed my little Pepita."

I parked my car, but left the engine running. A young woman I assumed was Lindsey Claire—her sweatshirt featured the name of a local Baptist church and a amateurish scene of the crucifixion superimposed over an American flag—sat on the front porch, the *Just Married* sign at her elbow, Zeke's gun and the telltale camouflaged zippered gun case at her feet. Her shoulders were shaking and her head was buried in her hands.

To no one's surprise, Cara, large and in charge, paced the yard and directed traffic. "Look," she said. "The paramedics are on their way."

"The paramedics are for people," I said. "Not dogs."

"That's what the dispatcher said. But I talked her out of it. Do you know she had the *nerve* to suggest this wasn't a real emergency?"

The young woman cried, a desperate sniffling wail.

"It's not your fault," Cara said. "Don't blame yourself."

"It's Erin's fault," Zeke said, still clutching handfuls of Ruby's bloody hair. "She's the one who left her sprinkler running. And in the middle of winter."

I had not, in fact, left my sprinkler running—and winter was almost over—so I wasn't sure what he was talking about, though I knew Ruby was obsessed with water and often caroused in the cottonwoods in the creek down below. I tried to imagine what must have happened before my arrival. A lover's quarrel, a dog imitating an intruder, a shot in the night. And why was Cara there? And who had turned on my sprinkler? And—I couldn't help it—would this brush with death hasten their departure and leave Zeke's land up for sale. I thought I should introduce myself.

"I'm Erin," I said to the young woman on the porch. Finally she'd stopped that incessant wailing. "You must be Lindsey Claire."

She looked up, her hair falling into her eyes, her ears red with shame. "You have to be on the lookout for Nazis these days," she said. "With Trump in office and all."

"Wait a second," Cara said. "You thought your own dog was a Nazi?"

"No," she said, again beginning to cry. I thought they were coming for my parents."

Cara shoved me out of the way and sat down beside her. "You thought *who* was coming for your parents?"

"ICE," she said. "My dad stole a car when he was seventeen."

By then the paramedics had come and gone. When they realized the dog was dead, they offered to help bury the body, but Zeke sent them away with a couple of pizza coupons he found in the glove box of his pickup. "Those guys don't make much money," he said. "These days."

Zeke went inside to wash up. Cara and I sat on either side of Lindsey Claire.

"You been helping out Mr. Higgins?" I said to her.

"Yeah," she said. "The lord called me to it."

"The lord don't always know what he's talking about," Cara said.

"That's the damn truth," I said.

"Don't say damn," Lindsey Claire said, and so I didn't. Later that year I helped her plant a garden. We tilled and planted and watered and weeded, and though I was tempted, I didn't say damn in front of her ever again.

Gift Registry

Picture books about baby animals or wooden blocks, a junior dictionary of foreign words and phrases: these were the kinds of gifts she would expect. But I was determined not to reward her tastes for what she called "infant citizenship" and instead decided I would buy gift certificates for formula, cheap cotton blankets, cloth diapers in bulk. How about a carton of various ointments and creams? If anyone's baby would end up with a bad case of diaper rash, it would be hers.

I don't hate babies, but I do hate their parents—most of the time.

Her name was Victoria, and she was pregnant again, this time with twins. We worked together at Lenny's Sandwiches & More. Her husband, twice her size and twenty years her senior, worked there as well, mostly doing prep work in the early mornings before anyone else had arrived. His name was Billy Ray, and he looked and acted like someone named Billy

Ray. The only thing non-Billy Ray-ish about him was that he loved the plays of George Bernard Shaw—something about a long-lost aunt who took him to the theatre when he was a boy. Other than that not-often-disclosed and not-often-indulged preference for plays pleasant and—especially—plays unpleasant, he was Billy Ray all the way: pickup truck, bad haircut, chewing tobacco, missed child support payments in another state. I hated him. How could you not?

Victoria's mother gave them a wobbling Woody Woodpecker high chair. They called it an antique, but everyone knew it was from a garage sale, not on their registry at all.

Billy Ray's mother gave them a diet cookbook, not for babies, but for adults. She was very into healthy lifestyles.

My own mother, who also worked at Lenny's—long story—bought them a microwave oven. They already had one, however, so they kept the one my mother bought them in a trash bag in the back of Billy Ray's pickup. *For later*, Victoria said. *When our old one breaks.* People had started calling her Icky. That's right: not Vicky, but Icky. Their cruelty was not without merit: she only rarely washed her hair. And she was married to Billy Ray. And because she was now pregnant, again, everyone knew she'd had sex with him at least twice.

I still called her Victoria. I had some decency, after all.

Clifton Crow, the general manager at Lenny's Sandwiches & More, gave them a bottle of scotch, also not on the registry.

Jason Jackson, the assistant manager in charge of scheduling, gave them a kitchen timer from the Dollar Store. This item *did* appear on their registry, although they'd asked for a much nicer one from Amazon. Every Friday afternoon,

Jason Jackson sent us all our scheduled hours by email. His email signature said, *don't limit your challenges; challenge your limits.* He really believed in all that stuff, too. He was always challenging his own limits, for example. Already he'd climbed Mount Everest, pushed a mid-sized sedan three blocks to a service station, and led a successful mission trip to Sierra Leone.

Jason Jackson's mother also worked at Lenny's. She gave them an oil painting of Noah's Ark.

By the time the baby shower invitations were issued, Victoria was eight months pregnant, still working, and considering divorce. I was the one who'd put the idea in her head, though I was aware she'd have trouble making rent without Billy Ray's paycheck. I had an old friend who was a lawyer and would work pro bono. He was not an especially *good* lawyer, but something was better than nothing, I told her, and she could always crash with my mom—or Billy Ray's mom, or Jason Jackson's mom, or, if worse came to worse, her own mom—if she needed to.

She couldn't crash with me because I was temporarily living in my car. I'd been sleeping on my own mother's sofa—another long story—but I'd decided at some point I needed out of there, and, at the very moment Victoria was filing for divorce, I was only two paychecks away from having enough money for first and last month's rent, plus security *and* pet deposits ready for a sweet garage apartment only a block from Lenny's Sandwiches & More. Things were looking up.

I was the fastest sandwich-maker at Lenny's, something Clifton Crow and Jason Jackson rewarded me for by way of always putting me on Sandwiches, never on register or grill.

Front register was reserved for Victoria, back register for a creepy guy everyone called Staple-Face, and grill for whichever "senior white guy" was on duty. All the rest of us filled in the gaps.

Victoria knew how to use the front register's microphone to her advantage. "That's NO lettuce," she said meaningfully, "Not a shred of lettuce, and I mean it." Part of the reason I was so speedy with sandwiches was because I actually listened; most of the other sandwich-makers would have piled on the lettuce by now.

Later, after the line was much shorter, Victoria told me Billy Ray had thrown a cast iron skillet at her head. He'd missed and hit the wall instead. I told her to take a picture of the damaged place on the wall, text me the photo, and then delete it. This conversation took place in front of a customer—a much older woman—who'd ordered Lenny's Signature Fish Submarine—plain—and a water.

"No ice," the customer said. "And get a gun."

"Don't get a gun," I said. "He'll find it."

"I already have a gun," Victoria said. "He gave it to me for Mother's Day."

"Shitty gift," I said.

"No it's not," the customer said. "Beats a vacuum cleaner. Even beats a robot vacuum cleaner."

"Have a nice day," I said. After the cash register coughed up her receipt, I edged Victoria out of the way, tore the receipt with too much force, and dropped it into the trashcan.

"There are two kinds of power in this world," the customer said. "The kind that men use, and the kind we take away."

I began to stack trays into a tower. "What if we try to take away their power, but they kill us first? With our own guns? That they gave us for Mother's Day?"

"Yeah, that's a problem," she said. "I hope that doesn't happen to one of you girls," She studied each of our nametags. "Either one of you."

"It won't happen to Lori," Victoria said. "She don't like men *or* guns."

"It's true," I said. "I don't."

"Got any mayonnaise?" the customer said. I always hated it when people who ordered their sandwiches plain asked for condiments later on. I also hated the word condiments. Everyone did. I doled out a large handful of Miracle Whip packets—even in those days of shortages I refused to be stingy—and sent her on her way.

Another baby shower gift: Staple-Face surprised everyone and gave them a baby-sized fork and spoon. When he found out they were having twins, he gave them a second set along with two tin plates he said had belonged to his great uncle. Because Staple-Face always kept to himself, most of us found this very moving.

"Get rid of the gun," I said to Victoria. Together, we were wiping down trays and lining each one with tray-sized paper advertisements. "I'm serious."

"That's your problem, Lori," Victoria said. "You're always *so serious.*"

"No, I'm not," I said. "I'm funny."

"Nobody really thinks so," Victoria said. "I've been meaning to tell you."

I was tempted to tell her that everyone had started calling her Icky. Because of her hair. And because of her sordid *preg-*

nancy. Instead, I merely shrugged and made up some excuse about needing to retrieve another bucket of ice. One disgusting thing we did at Lenny's was to use the same buckets for mopping the floor *and* refilling the ice bins. Sometimes we rinsed them out first, sometimes we didn't. These were health code violations for sure; I knew this and so had documented multiple instances in my files—in case I needed them, for later.

Wiley, the sixteen-year-old fry cook and occasional dishwasher, gave them a ten dollar gift card for Duke Decker's Sporting Goods Store. Ten dollars at Duke Decker's would buy you exactly half of an Aero-fast frisbee or maybe a water bottle or can of tennis balls, none of which Victoria and Billy Ray would really need for their new babies. But Wiley was a sweet kid; it was nice he'd thought to give them anything at all.

Always, it seemed, Victoria and I worked the same shifts: lunch rush plus the late afternoon lull. The customer who'd told Victoria to buy a gun had turned into a regular, pulling in almost every day at 1:30 to order her fish sandwich—plain—and ten-cent cup of water. It had been Clifton Crow's idea to start charging the ten cents for water. Before, it had always been free.

"You girls make good fish sandwiches," the gun-loving customer said. "I think they're even a little bit healthy."

"They're not healthy," I said. "I can get you a calorie count if you want."

"That's fine," she said. "Don't bother."

She worked, we found out, in the bakery at the grocery store next door. She didn't actually know how to decorate cakes, however; she was merely the person in charge of most of the overnight baking. One day—this was before Victoria gave birth, but after she'd filed for divorce—the customer brought in a box of cookies and offered to trade them for a power value meal and a frozen fruit pie.

"That's a *dozen* cookies," the customer said, edging the white cardboard box closer to our side of the counter. "Jumbo sized."

"What kind?" Victoria said. "We're not settling for no day-old oatmeal."

"All kinds," the woman said. "Every kind we make."

We knew Jason Jackson and Clifton Crow would not approve of such an arrangement, but we wanted those cookies; notably, there was no employee discount at Lenny's, and we were famished from having arrived early and worked through the lunch rush. Finally, while Victoria kept an eye out for any potential tattlers, I turned away and made the trade. Wiley, the fry cook and occasional dishwasher, looked up from staring at the bun rack and making slow circles with a rag—*if you know how to lean, you know how to clean*, Jason Jackson always said—and seemed, for a moment, to signal disapproval. I put my fingers to my lips and slid the box onto a shelf underneath the cash register. I'd give him one later, I thought, and suddenly he'd feel like a member of the in-crowd. He wouldn't tell, and if he did, I'd deny it. Oklahoma was a right-to-work-state and so a place where a respectable person was forever in danger of losing her job, but Lenny's was just the latest in a long line of low-paying gigs—I could always find another if I needed to.

"Billy Ray loves cinnamon," Victoria said, after I'd seen

her sneak a snickerdoodle into her purse. "He's coming over later."

"Victoria," I said. I'd taken off my Lenny's hat and replaced it with the fur trapper's hat I always wore in my car. It was stupid-looking, but warm. "We've talked about this," I said. "Billy Ray's only supposed to be there under supervision, right?"

"Sure," she said. "He's supervised. I'll be supervising."

"It's supposed to be his mom," I said. "Or yours."

"They're working," she said. "And after work my mom is going to Oklahoma City and his mom is managing a cage-fighting match." None of these things came as a surprise. Still, it seemed unwise for her to be alone with Billy Ray, even and maybe especially with their four-year-old daughter asleep in the next room. And Victoria was a sucker for his sob stories, I knew.

"I'll come over," I said, impulsively. "Let me stop for gas." I'd been hoarding most of my biweekly paychecks so as to solve the problem of my temporary status as one of the un-homed, but I had a discretionary fund: four dollars plus bounce protection on my checking account. The four dollars would get me enough gas to get to Victoria's and back, and the bounce protection would give me an advance of sorts at the grocery store; I wanted something decent for a change and decided not to skimp. Suddenly, I imagined myself crashed out in Victoria's garage—in my own car, of course—eating an attractive array of deli meats—on croissants!—relaxing with my feet on the dash and listening to Beethoven or Bach. Maybe some chips and dip. Nothing from Lenny's Sandwiches & More.

"Bring a board game," Victoria said. "Your mom has *Clue*."

"I hate *Clue*," I said. "I don't know why my mom keeps that crap around."

"Maybe *Battleship*," she said. "Doesn't your mom have *Stop, Thief*?"

"Batteries are dead," I said. "Everything's dead."

Finally, we settled on starting a new jigsaw puzzle of the Eiffel Tower, another gift, this one from Connie, who worked at Lenny's only after closing time doing deep cleaning, salad prep, and occasional fumigation.

"It'll be fun," Victoria said. "Academy Awards are on."

After I clocked out, I went to the restroom and changed out of my Lenny's uniform and into a sweatshirt and pair of jeans. Maybe I'd take a shower later at Mom's, the home-away-from-home I considered viable only for bathroom privileges, refrigerator use, and occasional storage. Most nights, I parked in the heated garage under First National Bank. The security guard was a gay guy I knew from high school. He wasn't gay back then, but he was now. As I drove, I felt suddenly wistful about this non-friend, friend of mine, this partner in crime. Would he wonder about my absence? Maybe he'd try to text or call. Probably he'd forget all about me and spend the entire evening in the toll booth eating snack-sized Snickers bars and listening to podcasts about unsolved crimes. Anyway, we had an agreement: I said nothing to his wife—also my old high school classmate—about his several boyfriends, and he said nothing to the bank's management about my illegal overnight parking.

By the time I made it to Victoria's, Billy Ray's pickup,

rusty and battered by gravel, was already in the driveway. I parked next to a row of leaning mailboxes in the street. When I walked past Billy Ray's truck, I saw his sheepskin jacket slung over a shitty cardboard box in the cab and remembered a long-ago incident at Lenny's: Billy Ray came through the drive-through during dinner rush and bragged about winning that very same jacket in a pool hall in Owasso. When I handed him his jumbo-sized Dr. Pepper, I mocked him for imagining himself some kind of cowboy western hero—I forget what I said, exactly, but the point was to take something he was proud of and make it seem small. Until that incident, I could tell he'd never given me much thought. But afterwards, his attitude underwent a notable shift: always when our paths crossed at Lenny's, he rolled his eyes and sniffed, not like a bull getting ready to charge but more like a two-bit donkey breaking out of a barn. Victoria told me he'd said I would never find a husband unless I found one who worked at a toothpaste factory. That I didn't want a husband didn't seem to bother him.

"Lori," Billy Ray said when he opened the front door. "We weren't expecting company."

Behind him, I could see Victoria and their four-year-old daughter—Estelle was her name—dumping puzzle pieces onto a low coffee table crowded with catalogs and kiddie cups of juice. Estelle was singing a loud song about stop signs and stoplights and Victoria was singing a soft song about God or Jesus or maybe both. The TV was tuned to celebrities walking the red carpet.

"Victoria invited me," I said. "To work on the puzzle."

"It's too hard," he said. "Fifty million pieces. And they're all the same."

I now regret what I said next. "I'm sure you're very good at puzzles," I said. "I mean, you have that kind of mind."

He stiffened. "I am good with moving parts," he said. "Cars. You know, machines."

"Sure," I said. "I can see that."

I'd had dozens of friendships just like this one: a woman took me into her confidence. A man found me easygoing and frank. In private, each one badmouthed the other to my non-committal shrugs. I hated these het couples for doing this to me over and over again. I hated myself for allowing it. All in all, it was a bad bargain, and I was its author.

While the three of them searched the sofa cushions for some missing border pieces, I stepped into the kitchen and waved off Victoria's offer of help. The sink was stacked with dirty dishes, a crusty, brown sponge balanced in the corner. In a cabinet labeled "picnic stuff," I found a plastic cup that looked clean and turned on the tap. The water dripped at barely a trickle; it seemed to take forever to collect enough for actual drinking. I scrutinized the walls to see if I could find the place where the iron skillet had done its damage. Billy Ray's damage. I saw a couple of scratches near the stove, but they looked like ordinary wear and tear.

In the living room, I made a conscious decision to speak mostly to Estelle, occasionally to Victoria, and only rarely to Billy Ray. The television was so loud I had to shout.

"What grade are you in?" I said to Estelle, although I knew this was a dumb, default question. At least I hadn't asked her if she wanted a pony.

"Pre-school," she said. "It's like zero grade."

"I'll bet you're looking forward to kindergarten," I said, dumbly.

"Not really," she said. "It's a hundred years into the future."

"A hundred years? That's a long time."

She sipped through a plastic straw, one of those "crazy straws" that makes the sugary purple liquid travel an impossible maze before it reaches your lips. "A hundred years is as long as it takes a galaxy to be born," she said. "Even longer."

"She's funny," I said to Victoria.

"She's not going to kindergarten at all," Billy Ray said. "Not if I can help it."

"Billy Ray wants to home school," Victoria said. "For a few years, at least."

"Sure," I said. "People do that these days."

"I'm not funny!" Estelle said. "Don't say I'm funny!"

"Okay," I said. "You're not funny."

For a while we worked on the puzzle. They passed out awards for best foreign film and best cartoon short. No one said anything when one of the award-winners, a French woman I didn't recognize, used part of her acceptance speech to thank "the survivors of gender-based violence in war zones around the world."

When they cut to commercial, Estelle said, "the world is really big. As big as the universe."

Victoria tickled her and said, "as big as a big bowl of ice cream."

"Ice cream is small," Estelle said. "As small as a mouse."

"Stupid conversation," Billy Ray said. "And this puzzle is stupid, too."

"You shouldn't even be here," Victoria said. "I don't know why I let you come over."

"Why'd you let your stupid lesbo friend come over?" Billy Ray said. "She's the one who shouldn't be here."

"Don't say *lesbo*," Estelle said. "Don't say *stupid*."

"You know what," I said. "I have some chips and dip in my car. I should go get those. Estelle, do you want to help me?"

"That's stupid too," Billy Ray said. "Stupid, stupid, stupid!"

"Stop!" Estelle shouted.

"I'm not going to sit here and be lectured by a goddamned four-year-old," Billy Ray said. "I'm going to Mom's."

Victoria said, "what about the puzzle?"

"Fuck the puzzle," Billy Ray said, sweeping pieces from the table "Fuck this whole thing."

Now Estelle began to cry, and Victoria soon followed suit. Billy Ray exited toward the back room and came back carrying a toolbox, a hammer, and a rolled-up sleeping bag. "My mom needs these," he said. "I need them too."

Victoria said, "don't you take my toolbox, Billy Ray. My daddy bought that for me."

He threw the tool box into the corner. The latch sprang open and various wrenches and rasps spilled out in a heap, scaring and probably scarring a Siamese cat I hadn't noticed before. Still carrying the hammer and sleeping bag, Billy Ray strode toward the front door.

"I want a cookie," Estelle sobbed. "No one ever gives me any cookies. I hate chips and dip."

"I hate them too," I said. "I was just kidding. Before."

"Go," Victoria said. "Get out."

For a moment, I thought she was talking to me. And maybe she was. Maybe she was talking to everyone. But Billy Ray got the message, and before they passed out the award for best supporting actor and well before the City of Lights became anything close to a reality on the surface of the crowded coffee table, he and his hammer—Victoria's hammer—were out the front door. No one even had to get a gun. No one even had to threaten to get a gun. I thought of a public service announcement I'd recently seen on a billboard across the street from Lenny's: *talk to your children about your firearms.* What if you didn't have any firearms? What if you didn't have any children? As usual, I wasn't the intended audience.

The next day at Lenny's was Victoria's day off. Staple-Face was on back register, and I was on back sandwiches. Clifton Crow, a true man of the people, told me to take a break, something he did when he was in a rare good mood. He was refilling the napkin dispensers and Jason Jackson was sitting at the front table working on the flash frozen food order when the woman from the grocery store bakery walked in with not just one but two large white pastry boxes, both of which appeared very heavy. Instead of her usual leather handbag, she wore a backpack, the kind with a metal frame.

"I'm going hiking," she said. "Robbers Cave."

Wiley the fry cook looked up from draining grease from the bottom of the fry station. "They don't have robbers there," he said. "It's named after some guy named Robert or something."

"Jesse James used it as a secret hideout," I said. Probably I'd picked up this bit of useless knowledge from eighth grade

Oklahoma History. "Back in the day."

"Got my power value meal?" the customer said, sliding the boxes across the counter. "My frozen fruit pie?"

I cut my eyes over to Clifton Crow, who, thankfully, was deeply immersed in solving the mystery of an errant spring lurking within the dark innards of the napkin dispenser. Staple-Face and Jason Jackson were both wearing earbuds, so I decided we were in the clear.

"Hand over the boxes," I said in a whisper. "Then go back to your car and pull up through the drive-through. Frozen fruit pies are in the back."

Indeed the boxes were heavier than usual. The first box, I discovered in the break room later on, contained three dozen chocolate chip cookies, more than several days old, I was sure. But the second box didn't contain cookies at all. As it turned out, this same customer who worked at the grocery store bakery *also* volunteered on the Labor and Delivery floor at the hospital, and this second box contained a sealed plastic bag jiggling like a Jell-O casserole, its weighty contents covered in a disposable hospital gown at the bottom of a bed pan. And although I didn't open it, inside the plastic bag, I found out later, still, was a human placenta. It was Victoria's. The baby shower was still several days away, but she'd given birth to her twins.

"She wanted you to store it in the walk-in," the customer said when she came through the drive-through a second time, this time in a different car. "So Billy Ray wouldn't find it in their freezer at home."

"You know Billy Ray?" I said out the window. Staple-Face had clocked out, but Wiley the fry cook was once again listening with what I thought was too much attention.

"Sure I know him," the woman said. "He was at the hospital. With their little girl."

"And they let you just *take* the placenta?"

"Nurses packed it up," she said. "I'm just transport."

"Why me?" I said. "Why did Victoria tell you to give her placenta to *me*?"

"That girl is troubled," she said. "I don't know."

I watched as her window buzzed upwards and she sped off into the distance. She had not ordered her usual plain fish sandwich and water, nor had she remembered her second frozen fruit pie. This town was weird; this whole state was weird. Trading boxes of cookies for power value meals was one thing, but passing a placenta through a third party smuggler was truly bizarre. Wiley the fry cook asked for a cookie, and I gave him one. I hated feeling like his formerly cool aunt, the spinster who could not be trusted with the knowledge of youthful indiscretions. Wiley was good natured enough, but I knew what he thought of me. I knew what they all thought of me. That I was reliable, but mean. That I was more like a man than a woman, but not womanly enough to work the register and not manly enough to work the grill. That I didn't have a boyfriend *or* girlfriend. That I lived in my car. That I could have gone to college but didn't. That I was lonely and my life was all but over. Why had I let so much time go by? Victoria, at least, had Estelle and her new twins. Wiley had his mom and dad. Clifton Crow and Jason Jackson both had wives and children and pets and houses of their own. I wanted a dog. A dog and an apartment. I was sure if I had those things, I would feel better, and sooner or later I'd be able to save enough money to start over somewhere else.

It was time for the evening shift to start, and Clifton Crow complained if you clocked out late. I let Wiley beat me to the office before making a break for the bathroom. After I'd changed into my civilian attire, I checked to make sure no one was in the break room and made my way into the walk-in. Technically, no one out of uniform—except for management, of course—was allowed behind the counter, but the dining room was dead and the evening shift people were crowded around Clifton Crow's laptop watching a series of what must have been hilarious YouTube videos. One could not see the placenta sitting on the shelf: it was inside a plastic bag, which was wrapped in a disposable hospital gown and floating in gelatinous mass at the bottom of a bed pan, itself wedged inside a white cardboard box from the grocery store's bakery. I pilfered a Sharpie from Jason Jackson's office—also the broom closet—and wrote on the side of the box. *Danger: do not eat or serve.*

I don't really know how to tell anyone anything. Would I be able to help Victoria get away from Billy Ray? Probably not. That ship had sailed. Probably they'd name their twins Billy and Ray. Estelle would stumble along through childhood and adolescence, drop out of high school and run off with some meth-head tree-trimmer guy, and Billy and Ray would grow up to be criminals. They'd go to prison, and then, upon their release, like Staple-Face and so many others before them, get jobs at Lenny's Sandwiches & More. By then, Victoria and Billy Ray and Billy Ray's mom and my mom and Victoria's mom and Clifton Crow and Jason

Jackson and Jason Jackson's mom and I all would be either dead or so old and infirm we might as well be. It wasn't a pretty picture.

Clifton Crow always told Victoria that Lenny's would welcome her back on the payroll—once the twins were old enough for day care she could come back and work the front register: no problem. But she didn't want to. She'd heard everyone had started calling her Icky, for one thing, and for another she had started home-schooling Estelle. Still, there was the baby shower to consider.

The date on the invitations had come and gone—Victoria ended up needing a fairly long stay in the hospital—but Clifton Crow was feeling generous: he wanted to close the store, and he wanted it to be on a *Saturday*, our busiest day of the week. My mom and Victoria's mom decorated the dining room with big, plastic baby bottles and blue streamers and balloons. Connie made pigs in a blanket; Staple-Face spiked the punch. Wiley brought a girl from his Biology class, and I'd invited both the gay guy from the First National Bank's parking garage *and* his wife *and* his two male lovers. I'd even scrubbed out all the ice buckets after mopping the floor.

Billy Ray, it turned out, had to miss the baby shower so that he could take Estelle to a long-planned matinee of *Major Barbara* in Oklahoma City. But a few days later, I ran into him behind the dumpster in the Lenny's parking lot. I'd just signed the lease on my new garage apartment and so was beginning to clean out my car. I dropped a trash bag into the dumpster and turned to look at Billy Ray.

"You should get a new car," he said. "I'll sell you my truck if you want."

"Pass," I said. "There's nothing wrong with my car."

"It's your business," he said. "But I heard it running earlier. Get your oil changed, at least."

"My mom took an Automotive class," I lied. "At the Vo-Tech."

"Good for her," he said. "Good for you too, I guess."

"How's Victoria?"

"I wouldn't know," he said. "I guess you got your way."

This was news to me. I'd assumed they'd reconciled. And maybe they had. Probably they'd broken up and gotten back together a hundred times by now. That they were currently on hiatus meant nothing of consequence.

"Good luck," I said. I don't know why I said that. I guess it made more sense than kicking him in the shins. When he retreated to his pickup, I realized he'd recently had his hair cut, and I noticed for first time he had especially large ears, like Estelle's. At the baby shower, Victoria had shown off photos of the twin boys, and they, too, looked as if they might take off into flight.

"Good luck to you, too, Lori," he said. "Don't take any wooden nickels."

"Right," I said. "In the drive-through."

At the baby shower, a couple of customers had tried to come through the drive-through, but each time the signal sounded through the speaker, Clifton Crow grabbed the headset and shouted into the microphone.

"We're closed," he'd said. "Private party."

And what a party it was. When Victoria first announced her pregnancy, people had been unexpectedly generous—something about poor people reproducing brought out these kinds of sentimental gestures. All those presents they'd bestowed upon them? They were for the entire family, even Estelle. But just before the baby shower, Clifton Crow—who long had a crush on Victoria; another long story—instructed everyone to come bearing another present. A single present. For Victoria alone.

Wiley the fry cook gave her his favorite baseball card.

Connie-who-worked-overnights gave her a new pair of slippers.

Staple-face gave her a glass vase full of seashells.

Clifton Crow gave her a bottle of expensive perfume.

Jason Jackson gave her a set of pot-holders his wife had made along with a bottle of spray cleaner he said worked wonders on stainless steel.

Jason Jackson's mother gave her a towel warmer.

My mother gave her a month's supply of Martha Stewart meal kits.

Her own mother gave her a candy dish made of carnival glass.

Billy Ray's mother gave her a jump rope and a pair of boxing gloves—size small.

The placenta-delivery woman—we never learned her name—gave her a T-shirt from the Robbers Cave souvenir shop.

And I? I was brave for perhaps the first and last time in my life when I gave her a hundred dollar bill I'd stolen from the front register when neither Clifton Crow nor Jason Jackson seemed to be looking. I was going to miss her around Lenny's, I thought, and besides, she was going to need it.

Please Listen Carefully; Our Menu Items Have Changed

The ghost in Miriam's garage was not a ghost at all but her ex-boyfriend, dressed in yesterday's brown work uniform—he was a driver for UPS—ratty house slippers, and a floral fitted sheet fresh from the laundry. He wore the fitted sheet over his head and, worst of all, he told her he'd used the sharp edge of a pair of needle-nosed pliers to cut holes in the sheet, for the eyes and nose. On the place where the mouth should have been he'd used silver duct tape to affix an oversized X, like the ones used by abortion protestors and people who thought you shouldn't pull the plug. That particular set of sheets was new, too, a gift from Miriam's father, a man who shopped at white sales, taught gluten-free cooking classes, and crocheted afghans, even though he was not gay, or not publicly, at least, since he was still married to Miriam's mother. And maybe that was her problem, somehow, that she'd expected Donnie to act more like her kindly domestic father. And now Donnie was moving out, after only three months, and, he said, cutting holes in her floral fitted sheet was some kind of last stand, a protest meant to force her to concede she'd been unfair, unreasonable to expect him to watch television programs about interior design, demanding to hope he'd come along to watch the flamethrowers and jugglers at her renaissance fairs, and downright cruel to expect him to take medication for his cat allergy or learn to live with the occasional sneeze.

But maybe she had been stupid to ask him to move in with her in the first place, since she was not, and never had been, what they called girlfriend material. She liked to do her own thing—she was used to doing her own thing—and she was not about to change at this late date. She was 42 and never married, and Donnie was six years her junior and already twice divorced. He had a son from his first marriage and a daughter from his second, neither of whom he saw except on their birthdays, or, more properly, the day after or sometimes the day before their birthdays, depending on whether or not the birthdays fell on weekdays or weekends. The collected pangs of this knowledge should have served as warning signs, but Miriam had never before had a live-in boyfriend, and finally having one, even a lousy one, made her feel more like a leading actress and less like the chorus girl she'd always been.

"You ruined my fitted sheet," she said that day in the garage. "You'll have to pay me back."

"I'm going to live in the garage," he said. "For a while."

Finally, after the stunned silence that followed, he admitted he'd lied about the apartment he'd talked about renting, lied about his new route with UPS, lied about working for UPS at all. The uniform was stolen, not by him but by a friend who had a brother who really did drive for UPS, and the women, he said, always thought the uniform respectable and cool.

"It would be respectable," Miriam said. "If you actually worked there."

"I tried," he said. "I couldn't pass the test."

"Get out," she said. "You can't live here."

At first he assented, saying the garage was too cold, for one thing, and for another he'd rather walk on glass than share space with the washer and dryer, not to mention the goddamned litter box. And he was sorry about the fitted sheet, he said, he'd only meant to scare her.

"Oh yeah," she said. "Like I really thought you were a ghost. Real scary, Donnie, just like in the movies."

"Not that," he said. "Your precious floral sheets. I wanted you to think I'd put holes in everything you own."

"Well, did you?"

"No," he admitted from underneath his ghostly disguise. "I lost my nerve."

She pulled the fitted sheet from his head and shoulders and wadded it into an unruly ball. She had liked those sheets, maybe not as much as she'd pretended to, maybe not even half as much as she'd allowed him to think she did, but still, she could not get over the injury to her personal property. In another era, she would have taken him to *The People's Court*.

"Look, Donnie," she said. "You can have the couch. Until you're back on your feet."

"That lumpy old thing?" he said. "I'll take the garage, thanks."

"You'll have to clean the cat box."

"Fine."

She realized she had the upper hand. "And fold the laundry."

"Done."

"And eat what I cook for dinner without complaining."

"I never complain," he said, which was a lie, but for the sake of expediency she let it pass.

Looking back, she realized the misguided vision of herself as Someone's Girlfriend had been both unrealistic and embarrassing, a false dream of demographic conformity, especially foolish in this, the age of same-sex marriage, children moving back in with their parents and vice versa, whole groups of young and not-so-young adults calling one another roommates at the same time they haunted urban landscapes and made experimental art. That she'd settle for a twice-divorced and now jobless deadbeat Dad seemed to her not just pathetic but diseased, a sign she'd read too many women's magazines growing up. And her mother had not pressured her. Her grandmother had not pressured her. She'd wanted only to know what it felt like, to be seen out to dinner with him, to wear his T-shirts to bed, to complain about his odd-but-lovable habits to her coworkers at the office. She worked in a cubicle, sure, but there was the break room to think about.

"How long are you going to stay?" she said.

"Until I'm dead," he said. "That's the other thing I meant to tell you. I'm going to die."

"Get real, Donnie. You're not going to die. I could get so lucky."

"The doctor said a couple of months," he said. "At the most."

"When did you go to the doctor?"

"Grubgeld-Decker Disease," he said. "Google it."

Later, after about five minutes online, she realized Donnie's illness was in fact a hoax, an elaborate phony news story invented by a mischievous group of medical students in Galveston, Texas, an allegedly deadly virus spread from computers to humans that made people—so far the disease had struck only Americans—sentimental and self-congratulatory, interested in only the blandest foods, keen on European travel, and pale to the point of translucence. That Donnie thought she'd go for it seemed insulting but also perplexing, since he must have known a few keystrokes would expose the lie sooner rather than later. But Donnie was always doing stuff like that, really, she should have known. There was the time he bragged about drinking expired milk that was in fact brand new, the time he subscribed to sixteen magazines using Miriam's credit card, the time he told her he'd brought home a surprise and then packed the freezer full of fish heads and squid. She might have called him the class clown if he'd had any class or managed on any occasion to make anyone laugh. Why had she chosen so badly? Why had she chosen at all?

But the days turned into weeks and he kept the garage very clean. And he'd found a job, seasonal work watering plants at a local greenhouse, the kind they dismantled for the winter and replaced with an empty gravel parking lot until spring came again. But when the work ran out he said he was moving anyway, going to Vegas, he said, where he had a buddy who worked the blackjack tables and for sure could get him in. Still, he spoke of his disease as if it were real, blew his nose constantly in a way that sounded fake, and, strangest of all, began to limp. All that would have been fine—par for the course, really—if something terrible hadn't happened, something totally unexpected, a cause for true and terrible grief.

Three hundred miles away, in Baltimore, a UPS truck hit and killed Miriam's father. He'd been in a crosswalk, listening to Shostakovich and carrying groceries home from the store, when the driver, tired at the end of an eight-hour shift, sped through a school zone and reached for the radio's knob at the exact moment Miriam's father took his first hesitant step into the street. The family, of course, was going to sue; already three lawyers had dropped by the house unannounced. Miriam knew she had to go home to her mother.

"You can't stay here," she said to Donnie that night in the garage. Donnie, sitting on top of the dryer and reading a celebrity magazine, did not look up. The air smelled of fresh cat litter and fabric softener; he'd been hard at work.

"Do you know how often two celebrities wear the same dress to an awards ceremony?" he said. "Pretty often."

"I'm serious," she said. "Something has happened."

"Not here," he said. "Nothing ever happens here."

"In Baltimore," she said. "My father is dead."

Donnie closed the magazine and hopped off the edge of the dryer. He walked toward her and, like a coach congratulating a player after the last big game, gave her a playful punch in the arm. "Sorry, kid," he said. "Rough stuff."

She went on to explain she didn't want him living there alone, not without her watchful eye to protect the house and her belongings. "You'll invite people over," she said. "I know you will."

"Not on your life," I said. "I'll stay right here in the garage."

"You'll forget to feed the cats."

"Never," he said. "Their habits are my own."

"You'll buy strange-smelling cheeses and leave them open and exposed in the refrigerator."

"Let's face it," he said. "I might do that. But I'll clean it out before you get home."

Something softened in his face so that he appeared at once compassionate and judicious, like a seasoned old gardener confident of an upcoming large and well-deserved inheritance. And his eyes were kind. Suddenly, she detected the scent of spray-starch in the air. Had he been ironing? She looked down and saw the floor had recently been swept *and* mopped, and the cobwebs in the corner had been replaced with a wide variety of brand new toys, treats, and cushions for the cats. He could not have been trying to win her back—it was too late for that—but his countenance was cooler, more mature, somehow steady and true.

"You can stay," she said. "I'll be back in a couple of days."

For dinner, she cooked something she knew he would like—seafood gumbo—and asked him inside for a dish of ice cream for dessert. That he declined and went to bed early was proof of his dedication to the straight and narrow, since ice cream was his favorite and the garage, that night, was fairly well drafty and cold.

The next morning, she phoned her mother first thing and bought a last-minute plane ticket online. She couldn't stop thinking about her father's injured corpse, the gash in the center of his chest, his bruised and bloody face. Her mother had identified the body without her. How many seconds had passed before he knew he was going to die?

In the kitchen, standing at the sink rinsing out her cereal bowl, she overheard Donnie from the garage. He was talking on his phone.

I know, he said. *I just need a little longer.*

A little longer for what? Probably he was late to work again, something he seemed to be able to pull off fairly easily and frequently without the greenhouse manager's notice or care. *I'm taking care of it*, he said. *As Emily Dickinson once said, "My little old life is like a loaded gun."*

"Please," she said aloud. "Mr. Shakespeare."

But something about his tone unnerved her, and she decided, at the airport, to call him with some pretend last-minute information about the care of the cats. She was checking up on him, sure, but she had a right, after all, to the secure knowledge of the safety of her own home, her own pets, her own washer and dryer.

But when she finished dialing his number, she heard a stern male voice, not Donnie's but something like Donnie's, the same allergic hum and cadences, but deeper and more deliberate. Surely she must have dialed the wrong number.

Please listen carefully, the voice said. *Our Menu Items have changed.*

Maybe she'd dialed her bank by accident.

To speak to Donnie, press one.

This was his number after all, she decided, he was acting playful now, like an older brother spying on his sister's after school cheerleading practice.

To speak to Donnie's Housekeeper, press two.

Probably this was some kind of a stupid joke about her regrettable willingness to allow her garage to become his living quarters.

To speak to Donnie's veterinarian, press three. This was getting ridiculous now; who was he trying to kid? She started to hang up when the voice was interrupted by a quick fanfare of trumpets, sprightly and majestic like the ones you heard on television during the Olympics or a royal wedding. She was about to hang up when the voice came back, louder and more forceful than before.

To speak to the ghost of Miriam's father, press four.

"You goddamned idiot," she said into the phone. "That's not funny."

She heard him laugh now, a slow, cunning whistle, his mean laugh, the same laugh he used when her interior design programs on television were interrupted by tests of the Emergency Broadcast System. She knew he was flawed, sure, but never had she suspected he'd be so cruel. "What's wrong with you?" she said. "You have something wrong with you."

To return to the main menu, please press the pound key.

"Get out of my house," she said. "Leave the key in the mailbox."

"Look," he said, now back to his real voice. "I'm sorry."

"You're a sicko, Donnie, and you know it. You've never even met my father."

"Really," he said. "Learn to take a joke."

"I can take a joke."

"Good girl."

"I'm not so rigid as all that."

"That's better," he said. "I'll take good care of the cats."

He hung up without saying goodbye, and she was left there in the airport, her hands shaking with something like sadness and something like rage, her suitcase like a dead animal at her feet, her head beginning to ache from the whooping sounds of a trio of adolescent male soccer players gathered around the small window to wickedness inside one of their phones. She paid four dollars for a bottle of water and waited at the gate, all the while thinking more of her father than of Donnie, though images of him in her garage—maybe he was sweeping the floor, folding laundry, changing a light bulb—crept around the edges of her memory. Maybe he was not so bad. Definitely he was not good, but maybe, just maybe, he was more complex than dastardly, more butterfly than moth.

At her mother's house, the mood was unexpectedly buoyant, since all four of Miriam's uncles and both her aunts had arrived in time to add personal, celebratory touches to her father's funeral. The brothers and sisters had grown up touring in a traveling theater troupe, and their general merriment carried them through all family occasions, maybe even especially the funerals. They told jokes and sang songs, made decorations from outdoor detritus, ordered takeout and fed the leftovers to the dog. Someone constructed a life-sized cardboard cutout of Miriam's father holding both a ukulele and a violin. They lugged photo albums from the attic, vacuumed old rugs, went shopping for mourning clothes in various vibrant hues. They hugged Miriam perhaps too many times. Even the funeral arrangements themselves and the depressing task of cleaning out her father's closet became reasons for long, funny stories that always ended with an anonymous brave act or someone down on her luck catching a break and coming on strong. In the midst of all the sad merriment and happy grieving, she thought only rarely of Donnie and in not at all generous terms. Something in the profile of her serious stolid mother refusing to cry during the funeral made her decide once and for all she would ask Donnie to leave upon her return.

But on the day before she was supposed to leave her mother's house for the airport, the doorbell rang and her phone went off at the exact same moment. Standing on the front porch and clutching his own phone was Donnie, clad in a black turtleneck and jeans, stomping his feet to keep warm from the cold. There he was, framed by the smeared glass of the storm door, his face unshaven and his hair sticking out in matted clumps. Behind him, she saw his car still running in the driveway. When she stepped out onto the porch, he hung up the phone and looked up at her with expectation and affection, a wish for approval like you'd see on the face of a poodle come home from the circus. How had he known where to find her? She realized he had all the passwords to her computer and free access to any old address books she might have left lying around; probably by now he'd drained her bank account and convinced the neighbors she'd moved away. From behind his back, he brought forth a single white lily.

"I was worried about you," he said. "Objects in this mirror may seem closer than they appear."

"You can't be here," she said. "The funeral is already over."

"I know that," he said. "An idle mind is the devil's playpen."

"You're not saying it right."

"Calm down," he said. "Continued use of that tone of voice may lead to cardiovascular events from shortness of breath, to tightening of the chest, to heart attack."

"You're not funny, Donnie."

"You used to think I was funny," he said. He held the lily at arm's length in front of him. "Before."

"Turn your damn car off," she said. "You'll drain the battery."

They all went out to dinner out at a pizza parlor, where, to Miriam's surprise, her uncles and aunts and even her mother all did inexplicable things like compliment Donnie on his turtleneck, buy Donnie drinks, and ignore Miriam's proffered conversation topics in favor of Donnie's. Now with something to prove, she agreed to forego her plane ticket and ride home with Donnie instead. Everyone but Miriam seemed to take his presence in stride. Back at her mother's house, she threw her things in a bag and issued her goodbyes. Not a single one of her relatives acted shocked or inquisitive or even protective, and their indifference made her feel evermore the loss of her father, who would have known, somehow, to try to scare Donnie away. Without him, she had a strange sense of belonging to the cosmos, so that pulling out of the driveway felt like pulling into a chasm between her old self and future self, a space so silent and removed you could not hear the sounds of your own breathing much less expect anyone to hear a call for help.

They rode home in silence, the steady thrum of the road noise their only companion. Several times Donnie asked her why she wasn't crying, her goddamned father had just died, after, all, what was she made of, stone? She told him to shut up and mostly he complied. At every gas station, Donnie made her stay in the car while he stepped out to talk on his phone. Once, when they were almost home, she asked whom he'd been talking to.

"Guy I know in Vegas," he said. "You know: *Start spreading the news.*"

"That's New York."

"*I want to Bee a part of it: Laaas Vegas.*"

"That's the wrong song."

"I'm the one singing it, aren't I?"

"What does he want," she said. "Your guy in Vegas."

"Very big doings," he said. He was wild, speaking very quickly. "I just need a little longer."

She finally managed to get out of him he had given up the plan to become a blackjack dealer and now was going into real estate, investing in a turnaround property in the middle of the desert. He said he needed to continue using her garage as his home base.

"It's my home, Donnie," she said. "It's my home base."

"It's a garage," he said. "You don't even have a car."

He was right, of course—she took the bus to work every day and walked to and from the grocery store—but she paid for that garage, paid for the washer and dryer and cat and cat litter box and ironing board and recycling bins that went in it. It was her garage, and she wanted it back. And a very small part of her—a part she didn't like to confront—felt hurt he didn't seem to want to give up the garage in favor of moving back into her bedroom. Why, for example, had he come all the way to Baltimore just to tell her he wanted to continue living in her garage?

Once again, she felt herself softening. "Well what are you going to do all day? While you're waiting for this magical windfall in Vegas?"

"I'll do what I always do," he said. "I'll wake up with the alarm on my phone. I'll check my mail. I'll play *Word Juicer* and *Mammary Time* and *Rat Hole Race Part II*. When my phone speaks, I will listen. When it gets tired, I will grant it the power of electricity. And when someone inside my little machine tells me something of some import, I will answer. I will answer to the call of destiny."

"You're crazy," she said, and before she knew it, they were home again where her cats were happy to see her but also happy to see Donnie, and, after a few days of unpacking and extra laundry, they settled back into their usual routines of seeing one another only rarely, and then with only muttered bits of practical wisdom and statements and false decorum.

Everything seemed to be going fine—she thought of him in much the same way she might think of a lawn ornament or a talking parrot she couldn't bear to give away—until he started inviting people over, and not just regular people, either, but children.

"I'm giving them piano lessons," he said one night at dinner.

"You don't have a piano."

"We're using an electric keyboard," he said. "Sometimes I don't plug it in."

"Do their parents know," she said. "About these lessons?"

"Their parents are *paying* me to give them lessons, duh."

"How much?"

"This is some kind of Jewish thing, right? Like you want your cut?"

"I'm not Jewish," she said. "But you still sound like a bigot."

"But you have Jewish relatives, right? Like some of your ancestors are Jewish? That makes you Jewish."

"You don't even know how to play the piano."

"I've been playing the piano, thank you very much, since the sixth grade. I went to a boys' school where they taught you stuff like that."

"I don't think you ought to be alone with those children," she said. "In my garage."

"This is a *business*," he said. "You wouldn't understand."

That she worked a full-time job and he was unemployed seemed not to faze him; lately he'd started reading stock reports online and tearing out pages from magazines featuring men in sharp business suits, aspirational photos, he called them, something to look forward to. And he'd professed, ever since she met him, to be an authority on everything from deforestation to the budget deficit to cheeses of the world. She didn't mind his armchair expertise, not really anyway, but lately she resented his need to diminish her own knowledge and experience so as to make his appear more worldly and vast. She'd been working her whole life, after all, always someone's dutiful Girl Friday. She arrived early and stayed late. And she had ambitions, too, it wasn't as if she took long lunches for hair appointments or filed her nails at her desk. She wanted something better for herself, something—or someone—than Donnie.

One night, she came home from work to find him sitting not in his usual post in the garage but in the back yard, at her picnic table, doing something with a long, wooden dowel that looked like churning butter. Looking closer, she realized his hands were fast in motion with not one wooden dowel but two, and they seemed like knitting needles, maybe, some kind of sewing or craft.

"I'm making baby blankets," he said. "For babies with no parents."

"Which babies with no parents? You don't know any babies without parents."

"You haven't been paying attention to the news," he said. "Haitian refugees. They need blankets."

"And you're making them? In my backyard? Another business venture, I presume?"

"This is *charity*," he said. "Have a heart."

"Since when do you care about charity?"

"Since your father died," he said. "I found the whole thing very moving."

She was angry now, unbelieving he would dare to bring up her own father's memory as an excuse for his increasingly odd and paranoid behavior. A couple of days prior he'd complained of cockroaches in the garage and, to discourage their mating, he said, put out metal pie tins filled to the brim with sugared water. When she protested, saying the cats would drink it and turn diabetic for sure, he dumped the water over his head and invited the cockroaches to "devour him like yesterday's dinner."

"I don't know why you'd go and start caring about people in need," she said. "You're not exactly Mr. Compassionate."

He said the Haitians would be coming over the next day to pick up the blankets, and he'd be hosting them in the garage. She thought at first she should stop him, put her foot down for once, but she reconsidered when she imagined herself ripping the blanket from a shivering infant and ordering the parents off her property. The whole thing seemed ridiculous, like some kind of high school competition to see who could collect the most canned goods. Probably Donnie had won competitions like those whereas Miriam herself had received her perpetual Honorable Mention.

Now she watched as he folded the blanket neatly on top of the picnic table and pronounced it finished. Standing, she felt smug when she realized his knitting was far from proficient. But why should she feel so small? How did this sleazebag always manage to take the high road? It was time for him to move out.

"It's over, Donnie," she said. "I think you need to move."

"Thank you for calling Rent-A-Center," he said in his robotic telephone voice. She'd heard it way too many times lately. She started for the house when he surprised her, saying, "For Hope for the Hopeless, press one."

"I don't like your jokes, Donnie."

"For Cruel and Unusual Punishment, press two."

"Enough."

"For the ghost of Miriam's father, press three."

"You don't know a goddamned thing about my father,"

she said. "So you can stop pretending."

But he was an expert now, a regular Robert De Niro. As soon as he started in with his telephone tree voice his whole body went limp and detached, so that his arms swung from his elbows and his head drooped toward the floor. But his eyes crinkled at the edges and his hand reached out to touch her shoulder. It was uncanny, really; he was just like her father. And he said kind and soothing things, like *I'm listening, dear* and *Let us together take some tea.* Like a two-bit player from some Psychic Hotline, he became a vulture and hovered over the smell of death. She had to turn away to keep herself from believing the lie.

The Haitians came and went without incident, and she didn't disturb Donnie for days. But one of her cats stopped eating and Donnie healed him. The washing machine broke and Donnie fixed it. Her windshield wiper blades went bad and Donnie changed them. Every night after dinner, he took out the trash.

"Is that all it takes," she said one night in the driveway. It was dusk, the whole neighborhood quiet with the evening news, the horizon a deep shade of orange. "You take out the trash and you're some kind of saint?"

"I take out the trash for the sake of utility," he said. "It has nothing to do with goodness."

"Have you been reading self-help books again?"

"I am the river and the muskrat," he said. "I am the wind through the trees."

"No you're not."

"I am the alpha and the omega," he said. He kicked a pebble into the street. "The beginning and the end."

At work, in her cubicle, she wished for something different, she hoped for something new. She drank a cup of soup and ate a cup of coffee—that's just how wrongheaded the whole upside-down world had become. Checking her email for perhaps the fiftieth time that day, she realized she was just the right (wrong) kind of person others expected to become a connoisseur of funny salt and pepper shakers, a lover of bathroom soaps in unexpected shapes, a joiner of book clubs. Everyone thought her the kind of person who believed all the stories about women who gave birth to three-headed babies and men who seemed at first like Dracula's wayward nephew, but became, through the woman's love and affection, phlebotomists at busy inner-city hospitals. In the stories, the women said plucky things like, *isn't it lovely? Isn't it just the love-love-lovely?* The women wore red lipstick, carried handbags that matched their shoes, and said to anyone who would listen they were *happy* and *blessed.* And when the magic happened, it was as if the curtains parted, the windows opened against the salty summer breeze. And the man was a monster. The man carried a dagger. He was a winged creature, a giant with hairy knuckles. He rescued you or ravaged you, didn't matter which. In real life, the hero was a regular old con man like Donnie, pretending for the sake of his supper to like and do all the same things her father had liked and done, teaching violin lessons to unsuspecting elementary school students, wearing a velvet smoking jacket to bed, ordering rare and exotic plants from catalogs, and now waiting for her to come home.

Guidelines

"You can change the guidelines to suit your imagination," he said to his favored children. They were not actually his children, though he treated them as if they were. In actual fact, they were his employees at BeTrue International, hired for their good sense and overall obedience, the hand-picked recent college graduates he always described as perfectly poised to take over performing his good works well after he was gone. For a long time, I'd known I was not among them.

We worked in an office adjacent to a pizza parlor, and always everything smelled of old mozzarella. Like tennis shoes long past their age of usefulness, the pizza ingredients seemed to fester and rot: never did the ovens warm to more inviting aromas. Perhaps it was not a pizza parlor at all, but only a refrigerated warehouse. We never saw a single customer. Every day through the thin walls of the office complex, we heard the sound of the phone ringing off the proverbial hook.

Usually it would ring ten or twenty times before a male voice—Sal's—answered and said, "No meats" over and over again, as if vegetarianism suddenly had become fashionable in our sad Oklahoma town, and indeed healthy habits had become (sort of) popular, or, at the very least, more popular than they had been in years' past. BeTrue International was neither truthful nor international, unless you counted a trip we'd once taken to Toronto, ostensibly for "kindness training," but really for a conference on consumer trends in monthly subscriptions and individual sales. The favored employees had enjoyed all the perks and none of the lecturing on that trip, and those of us who found ourselves forever on "the bad list" had not been able to transcend our resentment.

That day, we naughty children had been sent to the back to stuff envelopes. Why he still wanted to use direct mail in the age of social media was a mystery to us all, even his favored ass-kissers and sycophants-in-training. His name was Sam. Samuel Becker Trueblood. And he was bloody truthful. And he was truly generous. All you had to do was ask him; he'd tell you all about it.

"You can change the guidelines to suit your imagination," he said again. We naughty children turned to one another in disgust. Why was he always changing the guidelines? And worse, why was he always invoking *the imagination*? The life of the mind, along with truth, beauty, charity, and—strangely—*allegiance to the flag of the United States of America*, all had become common in the corporate lexicon, so common, in fact, that the mere sight of one of the infamous words or phrases projected onto the wall of break room meant all the cool employees—the naughty ones—were free to replace their usual surreptitious gestures of pantomimed choking and vomiting with public displays of exhaustion.

Stuffing envelopes on the floor of the break room—he'd recently had the furniture removed—we watched as the word, *Caring* appeared on the white wall next to the fire exit door. Simultaneously, we halted our envelope-stuffing, sighed, and shook our heads.

"Caring," I said. "As if he cared about anything but the bottom line."

"Truth," said Linda Ward.

"You know it," said Jean Key.

"He cares about his belt buckle," said Judy Davis. "I saw him polishing it in his office."

"Belt buckles don't count," I said. "They're inanimate objects."

"Truth," said Linda Ward.

"Don't I know it," said Jean Key.

Linda Ward, Jean Key, Judy Davis, and I all had worked at BeTrue for the better part of our adult lives. The favored employees called us The Ladies, obviously meant as an insult, but they covered it up with cooing and unwanted gifts. One of them had given me an ice scraper for my car. She'd wrapped it up and everything; it wasn't even my birthday. One problem was that it was in the middle of summer, and even in the colder months we rarely had ice or snow. Another problem was that I didn't have a car. I took the ice scraper and put it in the middle drawer of my desk. I did not say thank you, nor did I write her a note. I found out later she'd been my Secret Santa the year before, but had failed at the office Christmas party to give me anything at all. The ice scraper, inspired by her lingering guilt, had been meant to bridge the gulf between us. It didn't work.

The break room was suddenly very hot, and the old cheese odor from the pizza warehouse was wafting through the air conditioning vents. Sam Trueblood, his belt buckle shining like a golden mirror from Mar-a-Lago itself, entered from the hall.

"Your colleagues are changing the guidelines," he said. "From now on, you must stuff the envelopes while standing up."

"That's not very caring," I said, pointing to the wall. "I don't think they care about us."

"That's exactly the point," Trueblood said. "They care about your health and well-being. It's not *healthy* to spend so much time sitting on the floor."

"I object," said Jean Key.

"We should talk," said Linda Ward.

"This place is going to kill me," said Judy Davis.

On the wall next to the fire exit door, the slide changed from *Caring* to *Compassion*. "We do not speak of *killing* here," Trueblood said. "Let us speak of the springtime."

Springtime had been over for a while, and the lantana and marigolds in front of the BeTrue Headquarters had been replaced by the brittle blades of barely viable pampas grass. But talking about springtime was one of his favorite things to do; none of us knew why.

Just then, we heard Sal's voice next door saying, "No meats" over and over again.

"I'm going to speak to the custodial staff," Trueblood said. "There has to be a way to dampen the echoes around here."

"They quit," I said. The janitorial scandal had been a hot topic for days. I was surprised he hadn't heard about it. "Jerry showed a dick pic to Michelle, and they arrested him for indecent exposure."

"What happened to Michelle?" Jean Key said. "I always liked her."

"New job at Food Barn," I said. "She's in management and everything."

"Nonsense," Trueblood said. "How could our *custodians* quit without my knowledge?"

"You were still in Belgium," I said. "When the dick pic thing happened."

"And should I not have received written notice of his termination?"

"We handled it without you," I said. "The cops talked to Sal."

"It seems we should have a guideline in place to deal with these kinds of events in the future," he said. "What you've done—and what Sal did, and certainly what Jerry did—may be considered violations of our policies and procedures."

I laughed; I couldn't help it. "What would these new guidelines say?"

"*Compassion,*" he said, pointing to the wall. "Before contacting law enforcement, we first invoke the rule of *compassion.*"

"Compassion for whom?" Linda Ward asked.

"That's just the question our guidelines will address," Trueblood said.

Just then, one of the favored (younger) employees, the same one who'd given me the ice scraper, entered from the fire exit door. The fire alarm sounded, and we all covered our ears. Finally, after what seemed like an eternity, the alarm stopped, and the room went silent.

"You're not supposed to use that door," I said. "I thought it was locked."

"I have the key," the favored employee said. "It's a new rule."

"Look," I said to the favored employee. I knew her name, but always made a point to pretend I couldn't remember what it was. "There are no particular rules about who can and who cannot enter from the fire exit door. *No one* is supposed to use that door. Unless there's a fire."

"That's where you're wrong," Trueblood said. "Excuse me. That's where you're *mistaken*." The slide on the wall changed from *Compassion* to *Discretion*. "While I was in Belgium, the Guidelines Committee rewrote the entire handbook. They did this at my instruction. To criticize the use of the fire exit door is an express violation as well as an insult to the hard work of The Committee. I shall not allow it."

"Another handbook," said Linda Ward.

"Just what the world needs," said Jean Key.

"I'm not going to read it," said Judy Davis.

"I want to know what it says," I said. "Let's see a copy of this *handbook*."

"It's electronic," the favored employee said. "If you want a paper copy, you'll have to copy it down by hand."

"Can't I just print it?" I said. "That's what I did the last time there was a new handbook."

"We're no longer allowing printer use," the favored employee said.

"Why do we still have all these printers? What are we going to do with them?"

"They're being discontinued," she said. "For now, they may be used as platforms for approved decorative objects."

Once again, Sal's voice echoed through the thin walls of the office complex. "No-meats-no-meats-no-meats."

"It's really very tragic," the favored employee said. "My husband loves meat."

We finished stuffing the envelopes, and everyone was getting ready to head home for the day. Trueblood was in his office with the door closed, and the favored employee had retreated to the conference room, where, I was sure, she once again was consulting the other favored employees so as to make a rule against my very existence. I considered how I might tamper with the break room's hidden slide projector; what wonderful words and phrases I could project onto the wall! Jean Key would laugh and laugh. Judy Davis would bake me a pie. Linda Ward would take photos with her phone and post them on Instagram. We could start a movement, I thought, a workers' revolt.

Linda, Jean, and Judy left together through the fire exit door; somehow, the alarm did not sound. I reached for my purse from the shelf above the microwave.

"Not so fast," Trueblood said from the doorway. He had taken off his belt and was holding it as if he were some kind of snake-handler in a traveling circus. Slowly, he swung the buckle toward me, forward and back, forward and back.

"What are you talking about, Sam?" I said. "This is my purse."

"You're stealing," he said. "You're a thief."

"Compassion," I said. "Discretion."

"It wasn't Jerry who showed Michelle the dick pics at all," he said. "It was you."

He knew perfectly well I had neither dick pics nor a dick. I decided to be frank. "Why do you have it out for me, Sam? All these years, and all I ever do is pretty much all the work around here. What, exactly, is your beef?"

Again, Sal's voice came through the walls: "No-meats-no-meats-no-meats."

"My *beef*," Trueblood said, "is your indiscretion. Your lack of compassion."

"Do you have a guideline stipulating it's somehow *against the law* for me to grab my own purse before going home for the day?"

"There will be," he said. The belt buckle swung like a pendulum. "The Committee is working on it as we speak."

The next day, the slide projected on the breakroom wall said the following:

Charity: it begins with silence.

All day I was silent. All day I stuffed envelopes while standing up. All day Judy Davis and Jean Key and Linda Ward sat at their respective desks and used dull pencil stubs to copy down the tenets of the handbook from the screens of their computers. They did not speak.

The favored employee entered from the fire exit door and saw me lick my final envelope. She laughed and laughed and laughed. The slide on the wall changed from the warning about silence to a single word: *Joy.*

Coincidentally, that was also the name of the favored employee: Joy. She'd had it legally changed from Annalise. I didn't know why.

I broke my silence. "How come you're allowed to laugh, but everyone else is supposed to stay silent?"

"I'm a Gemini," she said.

"Right" I said. "Of course."

"Violation," she said. "Duly noted."

My college degree had been in General Studies, and I was too old to get another job. I knew I'd spend the rest of my days learning and relearning BeTrue's new guidelines. The whole thing was absurd, but something in me wanted to test the boundaries.

"Has Sam ever shown you a dick pic?" I said. "Or worse?"

"The guidelines forbid it," she said. "There's an embedded video that explains why."

"I know, but Sam doesn't always *follow* the guidelines."

"The Committee is working to establish a protocol for his removal," she said. This came as a surprise.

"But he's the owner," I said. "The *founder.* BeTrue is *named* after him."

"Surely you've heard about what happened at Liberty University," she said. Indeed I had.

I thought about asking her to consider joining us at The Ladies' Table, the place where disgruntled employees made our various plans of attack. I knew Linda in particular would not welcome her, however, and I wasn't especially pleased with the idea myself. Was she angling to take over? Did she have some heretofore unknown connection to BeTrue's Board of Directors? Would we soon be calling ourselves Be-Joyful International? I decided to play it safe.

"So your husband likes meat a lot?" I said. "What's his favorite meat?"

"I don't know," she said. "Steak, I guess. Why?"

"That's so unimaginative," I said. "Doesn't he like chorizo or lamb or buffalo or something?"

"Yes," she said. "He likes all those."

"What are the *guidelines*?" I said. "I mean, how do you know which meat you're going to cook and when?"

"No-meat-no-meat-no-meat," said Sal's voice from the other side of the wall.

"We don't have guidelines for that," she said. Her voice was full of something, not joy, but sorrow.

"No guidelines?" I said. "And yet your bodies remain fortified with plenty of lean protein?"

"That's right," she said. I thought she might cry, but she didn't. "I suppose we could use a little more structure in our meal planning, but really it's none of your business."

"Be true," I said. "Be kind."

"Always," she said.

"Forever," I said. And these were our vows to remain forever yoked to the good deeds of the good company, the goodness in our every word forever etched upon the blank slate of the breakroom wall. Sam never resigned. Joy never took over. I never left, and neither did Jean, Linda, or Judy. To be truthful, I never really wanted to work there in the first place. But after a while, I knew I would never leave. The guidelines forbade it, for one thing, and I decided, at some point, it was better to keep my head down and obey.

The Paper Anniversary

The paper anniversary is the anniversary after the anniversary of freezer-burned wedding cake, the anniversary for fireworks that might actually be gunshots, the anniversary for fondue sets never removed from the box.

If you people want to read the applications, you'll have to print them out yourselves, on your own time, on your own dime, loading, loading, loading; here comes the rainbow wheel. You're the ones who care about paper.

The paper anniversary is nothing like the paperboy, who's actually a paper man, not with a bicycle but a half-ton pickup truck. Would you like to donate an extra dollar to the Papers in the Schools Educational Program? I didn't think so.

Children—girls, usually—who play with paper dolls almost always leave scraps on the floors of their living rooms and expect their mothers to clean them up. Sometimes their mothers fulfill these expectations, and sometimes they do not. Remembering the ball gowns of their youth is like remembering the lemonade stands of their youth: flashes of brilliance followed by disappointment and gloom. Their mothers are proud of their daughters and their good taste in men. Their mothers want only the best for their daughters on prom night, wedding night, silent night, holy night, the night their savior is born.

The paper anniversary means you might get a book deal as a result of your high-quality tweets. You might sell more T-shirts to unsuspecting donors. You might make your own branding opportunity from an invention meant to make life easier. You might be thought of as charitable, bighearted, slim-shouldered, the kind of person who cries when she sees a photo of Dr. Jane Goodall.

Imagine the day when ATM machines distribute good will rather than paper currency. Imagine an ATM machine that pushes out pieces of pie. Imagine all the money to be made from the need for refrigeration: all those downtrodden members of the white working class, all those former factory workers, coal miners, victims of the opioid epidemic. Slice and serve, young man, slice and serve.

You with your leather-bound journal, your sentimental scribbling in a three-ring binder, your stovepipe hat and fake boutonniere. You've neither seen nor understood the latest ways to activate the network of opportunities that will deliver next year's hottest trending topics directly to your doorstep. Maybe you'd like to start your own business, a hotdog stand/home brewery/used clothing store called *The Chat Room*. Well, guess what? Write this on the back of an envelope because you'll need to refer to it later: you'll need paper for that.

* * *

The paper anniversary means you might get a paperweight wrapped in tissue paper. Your hands are too big to hold it with care. Paper train your dog before asking it to fetch your slippers and paper, measure for wallpaper, paper the house before opening night. As a home remedy, force paper bags over the heads of the breathless, throw salt over your shoulder, wrap your steaks in butcher paper and tie them with string. Draw a picture on paper and wrap it in paper. Affix a paper tail to a kite and watch when it refuses to fly.

If your report card came on paper it came in the postal mail, the box for comments left blank because you were so unforgettable in class, a real dynamo at crossword puzzles. You received an A in penmanship, an A in *works well with others,* an A in refrigeration long before it appeared on standardized tests. Your school mascot: Peter Pioneer. Who could forget the time you came to class five minutes late and refused to accept a tardy slip? Those, too, appeared on paper, and if you were lucky and needed to go to the restroom before lunch, you might be issued a hall pass, one of many hilarious props meant to make you return to class faster: a bowling ball, a piece of paper that said *Kick Me,* a fetal pig floating in a jar.

The piece of paper marked Yes or No is the piece of paper most meant to obfuscate, and the age-old decision, a checkmark or an X, is one you'll never live down if you choose poorly. Still, you're obedient. Have you ever joined a religious cult? Ever had an abortion? Ever stolen something from a convenience store? The paper pattern your mother used to make you a dress never turned into a dress. The prescription pad did not make you well. The poet died and left her papers in the attic of an academic building, where all the academics who hated her while she was alive now whispered of her papers, their paper-thin lips telling lies. The last time I wrote something on paper it was a list of crimes real and imagined, the terms of my employment, rock, scissors, paper tablecloth covering a flat rock for a celebration of books (Celebration of Books), paper party hats with elastics that snapped under the chin, paper plates in a landfill, what a waste to keep scribbling into the air.

Have you ever tried tossing a paper cup into a cold fireplace? Maybe you've written a cruel email from time to time and pretended you were *only trying to help*. Those recipes handwritten on index cards and meant to make nostalgia more palatable? You should not have thrown them away. The Supreme Court generates reams of paper. As does the legislature. As does the executive branch.

Polish it off with an insurance card kept in your glove box, stacks of old stories you cannot remember writing, printed-out receipts for three and four dollars, a copy of Melville's *Pierre*. You read the whole thing but shouldn't have, or maybe you should have; it's hard to say. Pony up for another coin-operated disaster, the weatherman pointing into the void, danger on the horizon, though it's harder to see these days; it's there and then it's gone, like those photos of you and your friends at the backyard wedding, one groom takes another groom, a bride takes another bride, and they depart to sign papers for the sake of the state and its new magnanimous embrace, great again, on paper, no one carried over the threshold, no one catching the bouquet, the women and their boyfriends holding hands, the men and their girlfriends holding hands, guests but not guests of honor, friends but not friendly, fortunate but not kind. To my love I say the following: let us load up the car and take the dogs to be boarded. Let us frame it or tear it to pieces. Let us read it, and name it, and call it our joke. Let us pass it between us, the ink barely dry.

ACKNOWLEDGEMENTS

Thanks and love to Lisa Lewis and Amy Cox. Great thanks also to Tony Varallo, Dana Curtis, Lori Ostlund, and Becky Hagenston. Another round of thanks to Toni Graham, Nahal Suzanne Jamir, and Connie Corzilius Spasser. Finally, I'd like to extend my thanks to the editors of the literary magazines in which these stories originally appeared, sometimes in slightly different form:

2 Bridges Review ("The Shark")
Arts and Letters ("Oh, I Know")
Bellingham Review ("Birth Certificate" and "Hospital Chart")
Change Seven ("Guidelines")
Confrontation ("April Fool's Day")
December ("The Moon Landing")
Florida Review ("On the Lookout for Nazis These Days")
Fictive Dream ("Envelope," published as "The Red Envelope")
Fixional ("The Old-Fashioned Way")
Gulf Coast online ("Shoobie")

Jabberwock Review ("Dress Rehearsal")

The Laurel Review ("Just Saying Hello")

The Masters Review ("Paper Fan")

Raleigh Review ("Please Listen Carefully; Our Menu Items Have Changed")

REAL: Regarding Arts & Letters ("The Quisenberry Family Singers")

Smokelong Quarterly ("Tabloid")

The Virginia Normal ("Photo Album," published as "Antifreeze Dream")

Yalobusha Review ("Playing Cards")